SCREAM FROM THE GRAVE

Joe saw a sleazy-looking blond guy lunge and pull Annie behind a row of cars in the mall parking lot.

Annie screamed, "Joe, help!"

"Help, Joe, help me!" She sounded like the voice in the recurring nightmare that so often robbed him of sleep. It was Iola's voice, calling out to him from a roaring ball of fire as the car exploded.

Joe clenched his teeth so tightly that he could feel his jaw muscles jump.

But this wasn't Iola screaming for him. It was Annie. *Annie* needed help!

Joe jumped into the van and twisted the key. The motor roared to life, and Joe headed the van straight for the struggling pair.

Books in THE HARDY BOYS CASEFILES® Series

#1 DEAD ON TARGET
#2 EVIL, INC.
#3 CULT OF CRIME
#4 THE LAZARUS PLOT
#5 EDGE OF DESTRUCTION
#6 THE CROWNING TERROR
#7 DEATHGAME
#8 SEE NO EVIL
#9 THE GENIUS THIEVES
#10 HOSTAGES OF HATE
#11 BROTHER AGAINST BROTHER
#12 PERFECT GETAWAY
#13 THE BORGIA DAGGER
#14 TOO MANY TRAITORS
#15 BLOOD RELATIONS
#16 LINE OF FIRE
#17 THE NUMBER FILE
#18 A KILLING IN THE MARKET
#19 NIGHTMARE IN ANGEL CITY

#20 WITNESS TO MURDER
#21 STREET SPIES
#22 DOUBLE EXPOSURE
#23 DISASTER FOR HIRE
#24 SCENE OF THE CRIME
#25 THE BORDERLINE CASE
#26 TROUBLE IN THE PIPELINE
#27 NOWHERE TO RUN
#28 COUNTDOWN TO TERROR
#29 THICK AS THIEVES
#30 THE DEADLIEST DARE
#31 WITHOUT A TRACE
#32 BLOOD MONEY
#33 COLLISION COURSE
#34 FINAL CUT
#35 THE DEAD SEASON
#36 RUNNING ON EMPTY
#37 DANGER ZONE

Available from ARCHWAY Paperbacks

THE HARDY BOYS CASEFILES NO. 20

WITNESS TO MURDER

FRANKLIN W. DIXON

AN ARCHWAY PAPERBACK
Published by POCKET BOOKS
New York   London   Toronto   Sydney   Tokyo   Singapore

AN ARCHWAY PAPERBACK *Original*

An Archway Paperback published by
POCKET BOOKS, a division of Simon & Schuster Inc.
1230 Avenue of the Americas, New York, NY 10020

ISBN: 0-671-69434-0

First Archway Paperback printing October 1988

10 9 8 7 6 5 4 3

Chapter

1

"Now, *THERE'S* SOMETHING to die for." Joe Hardy's blue eyes sparkled as he looked down the aisle of the restaurant.

"A pepperoni pizza?" his older brother Frank joked. But he knew Joe was looking at the waitress, and she was worth a look.

Ever since nineteen-year-old Annie Shea had started working at Mr. Pizza, plenty of guys had tried to get her to go out with them. But Joe Hardy was the only one who had caught her interest.

Girls always liked Joe Hardy. Six feet tall, blond, well-built, seventeen-year-old Joe attracted girls the way a magnet attracts iron filings.

His brother Frank also caused girls to turn and stare. But Frank Hardy had a steady girl—Callie

Shaw—and he wasn't interested in anyone else.

Joe smiled at Frank. "Can you believe I'm going out with Annie, big brother? Eat your heart out. When I'm around, she can't even see you."

"Maybe she just prefers children," Frank said, and grinned slyly. He took every opportunity to remind Joe that he was a year younger. "Sure you can handle a gorgeous woman of nineteen, Joe?"

"I'm trying, I'm trying." Joe returned his brother's grin.

Annie Shea *was* stunning. She was tall, had a great figure, and looked wide-eyed and innocent, as if she didn't know that all the guys in Mr. Pizza were looking at her. When she caught Joe's eye, she broke into a smile that reached up to her dazzling hazel eyes. Her coppery hair billowed about her shoulders as she approached the boys with their order.

She set the special pizza on the small warming lamp. Then she served a slice to each of the boys while continuing to smile at Joe as if there were no one else in the room.

"I hope I'm the only one you smile at." Joe reached for Annie's hand, but she was too fast for him. She spun around with a laugh and scurried back to the kitchen, ignoring Frank completely.

Frank was glad to see his brother so happy. Joe

looked as if he were really in love, for the first time since Iola Morton's death.

Before he could shut it out, a flash of memory sent Frank back to the explosion. An explosion caused by a terrorist bomb placed in the boys' car. The death trap had been set for the Hardys, but Iola had accidentally walked into it—and died in their place. Frank thought of the grim days following the incident, the days when Joe hadn't uttered a word. His brother had become a stranger, full of cold, hard rage and guilt.

"Hey, Frank." Joe waved his hand in front of Frank's eyes. "Don't take it so hard. I'll give you some of my tips on women if you want. You're never too old to learn new tricks."

Frank took a sip of his soda, swallowing the lump that had formed in his throat. "What do you know about Annie, Joe? This pizza job's temporary, right?" He watched Joe deliberately wrap strings of cheese over the tip of his slice of pizza.

"I told you already," Joe said, obviously annoyed. "She comes from out of state. She had a bad experience with an old boyfriend, and her family didn't amount to much." He stopped his staccato delivery and raised his shoulders once.

"But that's all over now," he finally said. "She came to Bayport to make a new start. She likes to hear about my detective work. She even said she'd like to try being a detective. Nothing wrong with that, is there?'' Joe had put an end to the discussion. Frank knew that his brother wasn't going to share any more right then.

He also knew Joe resented being grilled about anything, especially a girl he obviously wanted Frank to like. But Frank didn't feel comfortable with Annie. When she was around, his antennae went up. Something about the girl felt wrong.

Frank tried to ignore these feelings. He was a man of logic, a man of facts. But there it was—he just didn't trust her. Probably he needed a rest. Probably they both needed a rest. Ever since that incident with Iola, he and Joe had been involved in one case after another.

Joe, especially, had gone about their cases with a passion and intensity that sometimes worried Frank. He'd be glad to see his brother relaxed and happy again, Frank thought as he watched Annie toss a wave at Joe from across the room. Joe was concentrating on his pizza and didn't see her, so Frank waved back for him. But Annie frowned and quickly turned away when she noticed Frank.

Frank reached for a slice of pizza and tried to concentrate on the food.

Mr. Pizza, located in the Bayport mall, was always busy, and that day every booth was jammed. But even through the drone of voices and the clatter and thud of dishes, Frank heard the pay phone near the door jingle. A guy at the nearest table answered it. Frank watched as the guy put a hand on Annie's arm to stop her.

For a moment she stood still, with a puzzled look on her face. Then she delivered the order she was carrying and returned to answer the phone. Turning her back on the crowd, she cupped the palm of one hand over her ear and held the phone to the other.

"Now, *that's* popular," Frank said.

"What is?" Joe had his back to the pay phone.

"Getting calls on the pay phone where you work, especially at lunchtime." Frank nodded in Annie's direction.

Joe turned around. "Strange. Annie doesn't know anyone in Bayport. She lives alone."

Annie appeared to be arguing with someone on the other end of the line. The longer she talked, the more agitated she became. Finally she hung up and stood rigid for a moment, her shoulders hunched over, her fingers pressed to her forehead.

Spinning around, she started toward the Hardys' table. Her dead white face was in stark contrast to her flaming hair. For a second, Frank caught a glint of excitement—but then all he saw was fear, filling Annie's beautiful hazel eyes.

Joe half rose from his chair. "Something must be wrong," he said, his eyes narrowing as Annie hurried to their table.

"Joe, you have to help me." Annie sounded desperate.

Joe stood up and took the girl's arm. "What's wrong, Annie?"

"Wait here until I tell Tony I'm taking off." She started to remove her apron but stopped to address Joe again. "Say you'll help me."

"Sure, Annie. We'll help," Frank assured her.

Annie's eyes flitted to Frank and then immediately back to Joe. She grasped Joe's hand and leaned in toward him. Despite her obvious fear, there was something like excitement in her eyes. "Just you, Joe, please." Her voice was a frantic whisper. "Please!" Tossing her apron on Joe's chair, she strode to the order counter.

Tony Prito, the manager of Mr. Pizza and one of the Hardys' best friends, tried to tell Annie that it wasn't a great time to take off, but she wouldn't listen. She pushed past him and dashed into the kitchen. She returned with a black purse slung over her shoulder and rushed to the front of the restaurant.

Joe motioned Frank to sit back down. "Stay here, Frank. I know you don't like Annie. If she needs help, *I'll* help her."

Joe dashed out of the restaurant, following in Annie's wake. Frank was left, openmouthed and surprised at his brother's attitude.

Joe had to hustle to catch up to Annie, who was halfway to the mall's outdoor parking lot.

"Annie, wait up. You have to tell me what's going on. I can't help you if I don't know what kind of trouble you're in."

Annie whirled around and took hold of both of Joe's arms, staring at him with shining eyes. "Joe, you'll think I'm awful."

"No, I won't, Annie. Tell me. Who was that on the phone?"

"Phil Sidler."

Joe's hands clenched into fists. "The creep who—"

"An old boyfriend. Now that I've met you, Joe—well—Phil was the worst mistake I've ever made in my life."

"That doesn't matter now, Annie—"

Annie kept holding tight to Joe's arms, as if he offered the security she needed. "Yes, it does, Joe. He's here. Phil found out where I'm working. He says he's coming to get me, and take me away with him."

Before Joe could object, she continued with greater insistence. "I didn't tell you that he's insanely jealous. He'd fight a guy if I even looked at him because he was so possessive. I—I can't take it, Joe. It's starting all over again, and I don't know what to do."

Joe took Annie in his arms and smoothed her soft hair. "Annie, please don't worry. I'll protect you from this creep."

"Take me home, Joe, will you? Oh, my

clothes," she said, snapping her fingers. "I'm not thinking straight. You get the van while I go back inside. I left my clothes. I can't let Phil find me. I just can't!"

Joe took off to get the van. He'd take Annie home, then come back for Frank. Frank would be mad, but Joe didn't care. His big brother was getting altogether too critical lately, acting as if he had to take care of Joe. As if Joe couldn't think for himself, or choose a girlfriend. When Frank started telling Joe who to go out with, he needed to cool his heels. Joe smiled at the idea.

Slipping his key into the lock on the driver's side, he was about to step into the van when he heard Annie scream—quite nearby. "Joe, help me!"

He spun around and saw a sleazy-looking blond guy holding Annie. It looked as if she were shouting at him. All at once she jerked loose, turned, and dashed back toward the mall. The guy lunged out, grabbed a handful of blouse, and pulled Annie behind a row of cars.

Annie screamed again. "Joe, help!"

"Help, Joe, help me!" She sounded like the voice in the recurring nightmare that so often robbed him of sleep. It was Iola's voice, calling out to him from a roaring ball of fire as the car exploded.

Joe clenched his teeth so tightly that he could feel his jaw muscles jump.

But this wasn't Iola screaming for him. It was Annie. *Annie* needed help!

After jumping into the van, he twisted the key and the motor roared to life. He backed up, screeched to a stop, swung around, and headed for the two figures. He would pull Annie into the van and take off before her attacker could follow them.

Ahead, Joe could see Annie twisting to get away from the blond, skinny man. He had her by the arm, but Annie was strong and quick. She slipped from his grasp and stepped toward the oncoming van. The man threw himself forward and got one arm wrapped around her waist.

Bending over, she kicked back and caught his shin with the heel of her shoe. He held on, and the momentum of her kick sent them both reeling backward, out of sight between two cars.

"Joe!" Annie screamed.

As Joe started to slam the brake down, the man flew out from between the cars—right into the hood of the van.

Joe finished stomping the brake. The van bucked, and Joe flew forward, his forehead violently hitting the windshield. Through the glass, for one split second, Joe was face-to-face with the man and his grotesque expression of surprise.

Then a sickening thump sounded as the man's body was tossed into the air as if it weighed no more than a rag doll.

Chapter

2

"I THINK SOMEONE was killed!"

"That new girl who works here." Two people coming into Mr. Pizza were buzzing with excitement.

Frank sat for a second, immobilized. Killed—someone was killed? Annie—something had happened to Annie. Or *Joe*. Leaping to his feet, Frank slammed his chair onto the floor and dashed outside, pushing people out of his way.

In the parking lot the light atop an ambulance slowly revolved, throwing regular flashes of red light onto the crowd of curious onlookers. Moving closer, Frank saw the Hardys' black van at the center of the confusion.

"Joe!" he shouted. Frank pressed through bodies until he was close enough to spot his brother. He caught his breath and forced himself to speak normally. "That's my brother," Frank explained to an officer who was holding him back.

Joe Hardy was standing dazed beside the van, cupping a cold compress to his forehead. Two police officers were talking to him. One of them was Officer Con Riley, a friend of the Hardys. His expression was intense and professional as he questioned Joe.

Scanning the scene quickly, Frank saw two paramedics loading a body onto a gurney. Annie Shea, practically hysterical, was standing nearby with a policewoman on one side and a policeman on the other.

"Joe, what happened?" Frank asked quietly, nodding a hello at Con Riley.

"I-I'm not sure." Joe slumped against the fender of the van, continuing to hold the compress to his forehead. He took a deep breath and tried to answer Frank's question.

"Annie screamed for help. Just as I got to her, that guy—she says his name is Phil—flew right in front of the van." Joe grabbed Frank's arm. His eyes pleaded for help. "Frank, I couldn't stop in time. I couldn't help hitting him. Is he—all right?"

Con Riley shook his head grimly. "He's dead, Joe. I'm afraid you're going to have to come to the station. We'll need to go over the whole story."

11

"Annie?" Joe started toward the girl, but Frank grabbed his arm.

"She's all right, Joe, but I think she's on the verge of hysterics. Let the officers help her. They're trained to deal with this sort of thing."

Frank didn't want Joe going to Annie. Joe was in big trouble, and Frank couldn't help thinking that it was Annie Shea who had gotten him into it, accidentally or not.

There was nothing to be gained by staying at the scene. The police took the van—and Joe—to the Bayport police station. Frank went with them, taking advantage of the time Joe spent filling out forms to call his father.

"I think you'd better come down, Dad," Frank said. "Joe's going to need you."

"I couldn't stop, Frank, he just jumped out in front of me." Joe repeated this as he and Frank waited for Joe to be questioned. "I didn't mean to kill him. I was trying to help Annie."

"I know that, Joe." Frank put his arm on Joe's shoulder. He knew how his brother must feel.

"When Annie called for help, Frank"—Joe hesitated—"I, for a second, thought it was Iola. I saw Iola in the fire again, begging me to help her—"

"Joe." Frank gripped his brother's arm. "Try to get ahold of yourself. Someone will be in any minute to question you. Try to reconstruct what happened out there.''

To help Joe gain control, Frank went over the incidents with him, making him cover every detail up to the time of the impact.

"Joe Hardy?" A woman in a uniform entered the room where Joe and Frank were waiting. "I'm Officer O'Hara."

"Hello," Frank said, standing and holding out his hand to ease the tension in the room. "I'm Frank Hardy and this is my brother, Joe." Joe stood also. "I don't think we've met before."

"I've just joined the Bayport force," she informed them, ignoring Frank's hand and taking a chair. "Please be seated."

Officer O'Hara was an attractive woman in her early thirties, with blond hair, which she wore pulled back from her face. She studied Joe intently for a moment, saying nothing.

"I'd like to hear your version of this . . . 'accident,' Mr. Hardy," she finally said in a very businesslike manner.

Frank didn't like the clipped way Officer O'Hara said the word *accident*. Did she question Joe's innocence?

Joe repeated the story Frank had by now committed to memory. Frank listened for anything in Joe's testimony that might suggest a deliberate act on his brother's part. There was nothing. What had Annie told the officers? Obviously she was now in a similar room, being questioned as Joe was.

"Ms. Shea says she screamed for your help, Joe." Officer O'Hara glanced at her notes. "She states that she and Phil Sidler were arguing just before his—death." Again the pause. Officer O'Hara was painting a picture of the scene that Frank didn't like. Something was on her mind.

"Annie was afraid of him," Joe explained. "She'd just told me he wanted to take her away with him, that he was insanely jealous. She had moved to Bayport to get away from this guy." Joe tightened one hand around the arm of the chair and rubbed his forehead again.

"But she had been romantically involved with Phil Sidler in the past?"

"I guess so. She called him her old boyfriend. What difference does it make? She was terrified of him." Joe seemed to be losing patience. "Ask my brother. She came to our table scared. She wanted me to take her home."

Frank nodded yes. "She seemed terrified. But what does this have to do with Phil running in front of Joe?" Frank was ready to ask some questions himself.

Officer O'Hara ignored him. "Annie is confused over exactly what happened out there, Mr. Hardy. But she did tell us that she's gone out with you. That she's crazy about you, and that you appear to care for her. What we're wondering, Mr. Hardy, is whether you considered Phil Sidler a rival for Annie Shea's attentions? Maybe you were jealous, too.''

She cleared her throat before carefully wording the accusation. ''Maybe you saw an opportunity to get rid of this rival and call it an accident.''

Joe's mouth dropped open. He looked at the officer in total amazement. ''I—I—'' Standing, he straightened his shoulders, but his hands were trembling. ''That's just not true. You can't believe it is.''

Officer O'Hara studied her notes as if trying to make a decision. ''I don't know what to believe, Mr. Hardy.''

Joe was sure of only one thing right then. He would never have killed Phil Sidler intentionally.

Joe and Frank spent a lot of time chasing and apprehending dangerous criminals, but both brothers hated violence. And Joe knew he could never kill or even lash out at anyone because of jealousy.

Frank stood up and faced Officer O'Hara. ''Don't say anything else, Joe,'' he advised his brother. ''You don't have to answer her questions. I've called Dad. He'll be here any minute. I think we may want to call his lawyer.''

''Probably a good idea, boys.'' Officer O'Hara took a deep breath and stood up also. ''Since I plan to book Joe Hardy on suspicion of vehicular homicide.''

Chapter

3

THE BOYS REMAINED in the small room where Joe had been questioned. Joe was still in shock at being accused of deliberately killing Phil Sidler.

The whole afternoon had been like a bad dream, he was thinking. First, his girl was attacked by some creep from her past. Then when he went to the rescue—Joe killed him. It was an accident, but now the cops . . . Wake up, he said to himself angrily. This is no time to lose it!

Frank spent the same waiting time mulling over the facts in Joe's case. But there were too many things he didn't know, too many pieces of the puzzle that he didn't have. He couldn't draw any conclusions.

Fenton Hardy soon arrived, acting more like a worried father than a famous detective. He had asked the family lawyer to meet them at the station. The lawyer advised Joe to say nothing more about the accident and worked on getting Joe released quickly.

Finally, the door to the interrogation room opened, and Fenton Hardy poked his head in. "Let's go, boys, Joe's out on bail. What do you say? Home?"

"I can't go until I know Annie is all right," Joe said to his father.

"I'll check on her and take her home if she needs a ride," Frank offered. "She's in no danger now, and she'll probably just want to rest."

Joe started to protest, but his father interrupted. "That would be best, son. We need to talk." He turned to Frank. "The police have finished checking out the van. It's in the rear parking lot."

Reluctantly, Joe left with his father out the back door, and Frank went to search for Annie. He found her in the small waiting room near the front desk, where Officer Riley was standing and talking on the phone.

Annie looked up. "Where's Joe?"

"I'll take you home if you need a ride, Annie. Joe is going with our dad. She free?" Frank mouthed silently to Officer Riley through the open door.

The officer nodded, and Frank led Annie out to the van.

After giving Frank her address, Annie said no more. She withdrew into herself and hunched her shoulders up close to her ears and pressed her body against the passenger door. Frank didn't exist for her.

"Annie," Frank said finally as he swung the car around to head toward Annie's neighborhood. He wanted to talk about the accident, but he felt awkward. Annie had always tried so hard to avoid him. "If you and Phil were struggling and you pushed Phil away, so he fell in front of the van, then it was an accident. You can't be blamed, and Joe would be cleared."

Annie said nothing, continuing to stare out her window.

"You know they've accused Joe of killing Phil, don't you?" Frank said a little louder to the back of the girl's head.

"What happened out there, Annie? What did you tell the police that made them suspect Joe of vehicular homicide?" Frank had raised his voice and was biting off each word now. He hoped to scare Annie into revealing something that hadn't come out so far.

"I—I'm not sure, Frank," she said in a sleepy voice. Slowly she turned her head until she was looking out the windshield. She still wouldn't look at Frank. "Phil knew Joe was coming. He tried to get away, I guess. He ran the wrong way."

"Why would he try to get away from you, or Joe for that matter? A guy who'd fight anyone who looked at you doesn't sound like someone who'd run from a confrontation."

"I don't know. All I know is he stepped in front of the van."

"If you told the police that, why don't they believe Joe? Why have they booked him?"

"How am I supposed to know what the cops are thinking?" Annie said, her gaze concentrated on the side window again.

Frank wanted to probe deeper, but he kept silent. Annie was probably still in shock. Maybe she'd remember more later.

She lived in the worst section of Bayport, where the buildings were old and jammed together. Rents were cheap there, of course, and Frank figured it was the best Annie could afford.

"You can let me out here." Annie was unbuckling her seat belt as Frank slowed, looking for the number. She cut off the offer that Frank started to make of seeing her to her door. "I'm fine."

Frank shrugged and stopped the van. If Joe was going to get any help from Annie, he was going to have to question her himself.

That night Frank slept restlessly. He rose early to find Joe slumped in a chair in the den, staring blankly at an early-morning TV show with the sound off.

"Did you sleep at all, Joe?" Joe shook his head, almost as if to clear it. Frank turned off the TV. "Let's get some breakfast. Maybe we'll both feel better."

"I've gone over and over it, Frank. I keep seeing Phil Sidler, flying out and landing in front of the van. His eyes, Frank. He keeps staring at me. Right through me. It's spooky." Joe shut his eyes and exhaled in one loud burst as if he could force the picture from his mind.

"Joe—"

"I know only one thing for sure, Frank. It *was* an accident."

"We both know that, Joe, but it seems we're going to have to prove it. I'm heading over to the police station this morning. I want to go over the evidence."

"I'm coming, too." Joe stood up and followed Frank into the kitchen. Absently he plugged in the coffee maker.

"It's better if you stay here, Joe. I think they'll talk more if you're not there. I want to see the coroner's report and Annie's testimony."

"Annie," Joe muttered. "I have to see Annie."

"Not now. Wait till I know what she said." Frank used a no-nonsense tone of voice.

Joe tapped on the countertop with a spoon, then dropped it so that it danced across the smooth surface and clattered onto the floor. After he picked it up, he paced the long, rectangular space.

Frank took out a skillet, eggs, and butter and went about preparing breakfast. He knew one thing for certain—hunger wouldn't improve Joe's state of mind.

"Look, I promise I'll report back as soon as I can," Frank said as he dished up a plateful of scrambled eggs to set in front of Joe with a glass of orange juice. "Now sit down and eat. I can't have you starving."

Frank's first stop was at police headquarters to talk with Con Riley. Fortunately, Officer O'Hara wasn't on duty. Frank didn't know for certain that she'd try to stop his investigation, but he did feel more comfortable with her absent.

"Con." Frank spoke openly to his friend. "I need some help. You know Joe didn't murder Phil Sidler."

"I'd have my doubts," Con Riley agreed, tugging at his chin. "What kind of help, Frank? This isn't my case, you know."

"Just let me see the police notes, Con. Annie's testimony, the coroner's report."

"Well," Con Riley said hesitantly. He glanced around. No other police officers were in the room at the moment. Frank shrugged and gave him an encouraging smile. Con sighed. "I was planning to look them over again myself," he said in a low voice. "I guess if you leaned over my shoulder and caught a quick glimpse, it wouldn't hurt."

Con pulled Joe's file. He spread the papers over the counter, and together he and Frank went over everything.

"Look here, Con." Frank pointed at the coroner's report. "This states that Phil Sidler died of a blow to the head, a probable skull fracture."

"They've scheduled an autopsy," Con told Frank. "Something else might show up."

"Multiple fractures—" Frank went on. "And an opinion that the fatal blow to the head was caused by the bumper clipping Phil's head."

"Makes sense."

"No, it doesn't, Con." Frank shook his head. "Joe remembers seeing Phil over the hood of the van. He's having nightmares about eyes staring at him." Frank jumped up, spread his arms, and leaned into the counter, facing Con. "It's not possible. If he's lying against the hood of the van, there's no way a bumper can hit him on the head."

"How about when he rolls off? He could've got clipped when he fell."

"He approached the car at an angle—from the side—so he'd probably slide off that way. He'd fall clear of the bumper—I think." Frank added the "I think" so it didn't sound as if he were telling Con his job. Frank thought so fast and so logically that most people couldn't keep up with him. He riffled through the rest of the papers at great speed.

Annie's testimony wasn't much help. When asked if she thought Joe could have stopped and not hit Phil, Annie had answered that she couldn't really see.

"I'll tell you, Frank, Joe's in a tight spot," Con said seriously, stacking the police notes back together and placing them in the file folder.

"He shouldn't be, Con," Frank said. "There's something strange going on here. Did the police find out anything about Phil Sidler? Search his car? Find out where he was staying?"

"We found a hotel key in his pocket. And an officer went to his hotel. Not much there." Con showed Phil's few belongings to Frank.

A sports bag held a change of socks and underwear. Phil hadn't planned on staying in Bayport long. There was a wadded-up jacket in the bag and a sports magazine also. Phil's billfold contained almost a hundred dollars in crumpled bills, a driver's license—giving his age as twenty-five—and a picture of Annie. The snapshot was slightly out of focus, but it was Annie smiling at the camera.

The number for the pay phone at Mr. Pizza was scribbled on the back of a matchbook cover from the Bayport Downtowner. Frank knew the hotel; it was in the same poor part of town where Annie lived.

23

"Is this what led you to Phil's hotel?" Frank asked Con, holding up the matchbook cover.

"Yep. He'd registered there three days ago."

"Not yesterday?" Frank added a visit to the hotel to his list of places to investigate.

"See for yourself, Frank." Con grinned as he packed up Phil's gear.

"I plan to. Thanks, Con. Joe and I appreciate your help."

"Luck to you, Frank."

Frank glanced at his watch. In the confusion of the events of the day before and that morning, he almost forgot that he'd told Callie he'd take her to lunch. He called to ask her to meet him at Mr. Pizza at twelve.

Mr. Pizza didn't open until 11:45. Frank parked near the service entrance and slipped in through the back door.

The room was heavy with the smell of yeast and green peppers cooking. Frank found his friend Tony Prito in the storeroom, lifting down a restaurant-size can of tomato sauce. Although Tony was the restaurant's manager, he did most of the initial preparations in the kitchen and carefully supervised the chefs.

"Frank, good to see you," Tony said when he looked up and saw his friend. "I heard about the accident. How's Joe?"

"Not too good." Frank filled Tony in.

"That's ridiculous," Tony said, slamming

down the sauce. "Joe would never kill anyone because he was jealous."

"I don't think he had time to get jealous," Frank pointed out. "He'd never even met this Phil Sidler. Listen, Tony, could you give me some background on Annie? I want to know everything you know about her."

"That won't take long, Frank. I don't know much. She needed the job. I needed help. She seemed okay, so I hired her."

"Where had she worked before?" Frank asked.

"She said she had no past restaurant experience, but who cared? How much experience does it take to carry a pizza to a table? Now, if she would have been cooking . . ." Tony smiled.

"Did she seem different yesterday or the day before when she came to work, Tony?" Frank asked.

Tony thought about that while he opened a cardboard barrel of flour. "Well, Annie wasn't a chatterer, didn't say much at all. Last couple of days, though, she talked a blue streak."

"About what?"

"Nothing in particular. You know how girls can yap on and on about nothing at all. She had the other girls laughing a couple of times. Probably doesn't mean anything, but I noticed it."

"Thanks, Tony." Frank turned to leave.

Tony stopped him with his voice. "Let me know if there's anything I can do for Joe."

"Will do." Frank headed out to the restaurant through the kitchen.

Callie was waiting for him in the entryway. "I don't know why I put up with you, Frank. You invite me out to lunch at twelve and then aren't here on time. We could have made it for a later time."

"Hi to you, too, Callie," Frank said. "You're a patient woman. Listen, do you mind if we eat someplace else? I can't face pizza today."

"Sure, Frank. But what's wrong? We eat here so often, I thought you liked only pizza."

Frank filled Callie in as they got seated at a sandwich bar in a corner of the mall's eating area.

"Joe's been accused of murder?" Callie's face registered her astonishment. "How can that be? When did this happen?"

"Yesterday. You must not have seen the news last night or today's paper. The *Bayport News* made a big deal out of the son of Fenton Hardy being involved in a vehicular homicide."

Frank gave Callie the rest of the details as they ate. "There's something wrong here, Callie. I'd like to know what Annie really saw."

"You're being kind of hard on Annie, Frank," Callie answered. "You may not like her, but you have to give her the benefit of the doubt. I think you're trying to make a mystery where none exists. What Joe needs is a decent lawyer, not a detective looking for motives that aren't there.''

"Yeah, I keep telling myself that. Maybe I need a vacation.'' Frank smiled at the pretty blond girl sitting opposite him. He watched as she echoed his smile by lifting the edges of her mouth in a slow grin that spread infectiously up to her understanding eyes. Callie was the world's most patient and understanding friend. Frank felt lucky that she put up with him.

"Listen, Callie,'' he said, polishing off a hamburger. "I've got some more ground to cover. Will you forgive me if I run?''

"Don't I always?'' Callie said, deciding at the last minute to make it a joke.

Frank smiled and sketched a quick wave as he dashed out. Maybe he *was* inventing this case, but he was determined to check out every angle for Joe's sake. Callie was right in saying a good lawyer could get Joe off, but Frank didn't want Joe to be left dealing with another guilt trip. Frank didn't even know what he was looking for at this point, but he was going to investigate every detail.

The Bayport Downtowner was once in the heart of Bayport, but the center of the city's activities had moved. The neighborhood had been left to change with the times. Trouble was, it hadn't changed for the better.

Half the fluorescent tubes in the fixture in the entrance of the cheap hotel were broken. The windowpane in the main door was cracked, and the door itself stuck when Frank tugged on it.

Behind the counter a clerk nodded sleepily in the dusty air of the lobby, air that had trapped stale cigar smoke. Two elderly men sat in a lobby off the entryway, watching a game show on TV.

"Ahem." Frank cleared his throat to alert the clerk that he had a potential customer.

"Oh, hello. Want a room?" The man behind the desk was past retirement age, and Frank figured he'd taken the job to have something to do. The salary couldn't be much.

"Can you tell me what room Phil Sidler is in?" Frank asked for starters.

"Unfortunately, Mr. Sidler doesn't reside here anymore." The clerk flashed a toothless grin.

"Okay, what room did he have when he did live here?" Frank found he didn't have his usual patience with people.

"Won't do me any good to tell you. Police have it sealed off. Why do you want to know? Was Sidler a friend of yours? Police might want to talk to you." The old man wasn't dumb.

"A friend of mine thought she left her purse in his room. I said I'd get it back for her." It was a clumsy story but the best Frank could come up with on the spur of the moment.

"Cops took everything." The man relented for

a moment as he added, "Two-oh-nine, second floor, corner. But you'd better try the police station, sonny." The clerk, tired of acting important, walked over to the small lobby full of faded easy chairs and joined the two men watching the game show.

Frank hesitated. The clerk really didn't seem to care if he went up for a look. He glanced around to make sure no one was watching, then quietly he took the stairs two at a time. Upstairs, Frank read the police notice on Phil's room and turned the knob once. The door was locked.

Disappointed, he slipped back downstairs and out the building. He stood on the sidewalk for a moment, looking up at the grimy facade of the hotel.

Suddenly Frank realized that the rusty fire escape must be right outside the corner room. He found a couple of wooden crates left in a nearby alley. He piled the crates up in a shaky tower beneath the fire escape and climbed it. He was almost able to reach the bottom rung of the ladder, which hung down from the second-floor landing.

As Frank jumped up to grab the ladder, the crates collapsed with a loud crash. For a moment he swung helplessly in empty space, one hand clutching the metal rung, waiting for someone to come out to see what was going on. But no one bothered.

Instead, the rusty ladder began slowly to ease down under his weight until Frank could climb it up to Phil's window. His sneakers muffled his footsteps, but the metal creaked and rattled with each step and once even banged against the building.

Standing outside what he was sure had to be Phil's room, Frank glanced about before trying the window. A matchbook cover was wedged into the space between the metal railing and the building. Two cigarette butts had been ground out on the railing. Frank could imagine someone leaning against the building, smoking and absentmindedly pushing the cardboard cover into the small space.

The advertisement on the match cover was for a bar in New York City. It might mean nothing, it might have been left there long ago, but Frank stuck it into his pants pocket to investigate at a later time.

The window to Phil's room was unlocked and open, two or three inches. So much for sealed rooms, Frank thought. But after raising the window and stepping into the room, Frank knew that the police weren't the only ones to have been there.

He quickly closed the venetian blinds so no one could see him in the room. The place was a shambles. Chairs had been overturned; upholstery had been slit; the mattress was in shreds.

Someone had done a very thorough job searching Phil Sidler's room.

Frank was reaching for the light switch to have a better look when he heard the click of the door lock. He started to whirl around to hide, but there was no time to move. The doorknob turned. Frank's only impression was that the man who entered was tall.

"What the—" the man cried. His reactions were lightning fast. He raised his arm to deliver a blow.

Before Frank could reach out to protect himself, he was sent spinning into gaping blackness.

Chapter

4

FRANK HAD DUCKED so that the blow only glanced off his skull. But it did momentarily make him black out—enough to keep him from identifying the man later. All he knew was that the man was very tall—and agile. Shaking his head once, Frank looked around and saw he was alone. He staggered out into the hallway and recovered enough to weave down the stairs.

Out on the street he looked both ways. An elderly woman was making her way slowly toward the corner of the block. A tomcat, scarred from many battles, looked back at him before rolling his back once and moving on. But no tall man. The man had been unbelievably quick. He had reacted to seeing Frank in the room in a fraction of a second. Who was he?

Frank knew it wasn't logical that he was the same person who had ransacked the room earlier. The search had been thorough enough not to be continued or repeated. And how did the man get into Phil's room? It seemed that he had a key. Had Phil been accompanied to Bayport?

The hotel clerk had disappeared, so Frank didn't bother to find and question him about the stranger. He'd probably gone out for coffee, Frank decided. Tight security in this place.

There was no way of knowing where the tall man had gone, why he had been there in the first place, or whether he might return. But Frank didn't want to leave without checking out Phil's room. He might not get a second chance.

Frank gently probed the spot on his head where he'd been hit. He could feel an egg forming, but at least he wasn't bleeding. He decided to take one more chance.

He slipped back up the stairs and into Phil's room. This time it remained empty. Frank searched for a few minutes. Nothing. It was pure luck that Frank had turned up that matchbook cover on the fire escape. Of course, it could have belonged to a previous occupant. The month had been dry, so the condition of the cover would have remained the same for several weeks.

After climbing down the fire escape—just in case the hotel clerk had returned to his post—

Frank got in the van and headed for home. He needed to talk to his father and Joe.

"Where's Dad?" asked Frank, striding into the den.

Joe was slumped in a chair, dully watching an old movie on television. Mr. Hardy had insisted that Joe stay in the house because he was only out on bail. Fenton Hardy knew Joe could get in trouble and then the police would have no choice but to lock him up.

"He left for the police station right after he told me not to leave the house for the tenth time." Joe followed Frank into the kitchen. "What did you find out, Frank? And where have you been?"

"Police station. Nothing new." Frank debated whether or not to tell Joe about the incident in Phil's room but chose to keep it to himself in case Joe decided to investigate.

"Well, I've had it with sitting around, Frank. I've got to find out where Annie is and whether she's okay." He started to pace the kitchen. "I've been calling her place all day and there's no answer."

"I can see you've been worried," Frank said, staring into the open refrigerator. "No milk, no ice cream. Where's the chocolate cake Aunt Gertrude made yesterday?"

Joe grinned, almost like his old self. "That'll teach you to leave me here alone."

"You ate the whole thing?" Frank muttered, not believing it. "It's only four-thirty."

"Frank, give me my keys to the van. I'll stop at a bakery on the way back from checking on Annie." Joe's grin vanished.

Frank had used Joe's keys when they had driven to the police station after the accident. He had conveniently kept them. Just telling Joe to stay at home would never work for long—no matter who gave the order. While Joe might not directly disobey his father, he had always made up creative excuses for "forgetting."

"I'll go with you," Frank said. "Let me go to the station and talk to Dad, then I'll come right back and we'll find Annie."

"Stop treating me like a kid, Frank." Joe tried to stick his hand into Frank's pocket, and the two scuffled.

"Boys!" Gertrude Hardy, the Hardys' aunt and baker of the consumed chocolate cake, appeared in the doorway. "Every time I think the two of you have grown up, I find you acting like children. If you want to wrestle, please go outside."

Frank grinned at the scolding. It was good to see his aunt back to her old self. One of the boys' cases had revolved around their aunt's being falsely accused of murder. Frank suddenly realized that now a second member of the Hardy household was in the same circumstances. He glanced at Joe, who was staring longingly out the window as if he were jailed.

"I hope you're going to start dinner early, Aunt Gertrude," said Frank. "I'm starved, and this human garbage disposal has emptied the kitchen in one afternoon."

"I'll start supper soon. Oh, by the way, your father called. He said to tell you that neither of you is to leave the house until he comes home. He wants to talk to both of you."

Frank was glad to have his father back up his opinion—for the eleventh time—that Joe should stay put. He exchanged a glance with his brother and checked his pocket for Joe's car keys, then settled for an apple to hold him till dinner. He went up to his room to think.

Dinner was quiet, with each member of the Hardy family caught up in his or her own thoughts. Finally Mrs. Hardy spoke. "Fenton, what's the latest on Joe's case?"

Mr. Hardy looked at both Joe and Frank. Frank got the idea his father didn't want to discuss this matter at the dinner table.

"Officer O'Hara is unbendable," Mr. Hardy said, pushing away his half-eaten dinner. "I think my 'unofficial connection' to the department is hurting you, Joe. I'm sorry. She doesn't want anyone to think she's playing favorites by letting you off easily."

Aunt Gertrude frowned, then harumphed.

"Surely no one else down there thinks our Joe could run over someone deliberately."

"Women," Joe scoffed, unable to resist baiting his aunt. "Why the Bayport Police Department thought they had to hire a woman is beyond me."

Joe's mock-chauvinistic attitude set everyone laughing. It was a relief. This was one family that needed a laugh.

Aunt Gertrude, who had argued equal rights for women for years, pretended to be offended by Joe's remarks. "Are you saying that women don't make good detectives?"

Joe grinned and helped himself to Aunt Gertrude's apple pie. "I think they make better cooks."

"I refuse to contribute to this discussion on any grounds I can come up with." Fenton Hardy smiled, filled his coffee cup, and headed for his study.

While Joe started in on the pie, Frank excused himself and followed his father. "I checked out Phil Sidler's hotel room, Dad." Frank told his father what had happened there.

The fact that Phil's room had been searched and that someone wanted his identity kept secret told Frank there was more going on in the case than a simple automobile accident.

His father confirmed his opinion, and then tried to stop Frank's investigation.

"Frank, I got some more information late this

afternoon. The police checked out Phil Sidler. He's a strong suspect in a recent diamond robbery in New York. The robbery looked like it was related to a number of similar crimes around the state. There's a strong connection to one gang.''

"Then they think Phil Sidler was a member of this gang?" Frank gingerly rubbed the back of his head where the lump was now perfectly formed.

"Yes, and, Frank—" Fenton Hardy got up from his desk and walked over to the window, looking out. He was silent for a while.

"What is it, Dad?" Frank asked, breaking the quiet.

Mr. Hardy swung around and walked back to face Frank. "The New York district attorney's office is claiming that Annie Shea might also be part of this gang. I think O'Hara believes that Annie got Joe involved."

Chapter

5

"THAT'S CRAZY," FRANK SAID, getting to his feet. "What's with that woman? How could she possibly think Joe's a thief!"

"Calm down, Frank. She doesn't know Joe. And our getting angry at her won't help him any. Although I have to admit that I had the same reaction at the station."

"I didn't tell Joe about going to Phil's room and about it being searched. I don't like keeping secrets from him. Do you think we should tell him about Annie?"

"I don't know, Frank. I guess we both know what he'd say."

"Let's sleep on it, Dad." Frank headed for his room. "A thief *and* a murderer!" he muttered. "Perfectly dumb."

In the morning, when he and Joe were eating their late breakfast, Frank decided to tell Joe everything. After all, Joe had everything at stake, and Frank was beginning to feel that he needed his partner to help him.

"Joe, I have some bad news," Frank said, buttering his toast and spreading Aunt Gertrude's homemade strawberry jam on top.

"Shoot. I'm getting used to it." Joe polished off a second glass of milk.

"The police on the Sidler case suspect Phil of being part of a recent diamond heist. It seems he might have been part of a gang."

"So I found a criminal for them. Maybe now they'll thank me instead of accusing me of murder." Joe's tone of voice suggested his depression had turned to anger.

"Joe . . ." Frank hesitated. There was only one way to tell Joe this—straight. "Joe, the cops have heard from the New York DA's office. They think Annie might be part of the gang."

Joe stared at Frank in disbelief. "You'll think up anything to get at Annie, won't you, Frank? I know you don't like her, but I never thought you'd say anything like this."

"I didn't make it up, Joe. Call Dad. Call the police department. Talk to Con," he said quietly and evenly.

"I'll do better than that." Joe pushed away

from the table. "I'll ask Annie. She'll tell me the truth."

"I'm going with you to look for her, Joe."

"Not if you're going to accuse her of being a crook."

"Joe, I don't know what's going on here any more than you do. I have no idea if Annie is guilty or innocent. I'm just telling you what Dad told me. But I don't want you to be alone. I don't want anything to happen so O'Hara will have an excuse to lock you up."

Joe studied Frank's face. Finally he said, "Okay, big brother, looks like I'm stuck with you. Let's go."

The Hardys first drove to Mr. Pizza to see if Annie would be coming in that day. Joe's face was grim as they approached the back door.

"Hey, Tony," Joe said as they walked into the kitchen, where Tony Prito was dumping flour in a large bowl to make dough. "Annie around?"

"Joe, sorry about your troubles," Tony said, greeting the Hardys after turning on the mixer. "Let's move away from the noise," he said, and strolled over to a corner. "Annie won't be in today. But, well, she was here earlier. She sneaked in during the night and slept in the back room."

"She *slept* here last night?" Joe didn't know what to make of this news. "Why?"

"This morning when I found her she asked me

not to tell you. But under the circumstances, I think you should know. She's scared, Joe, really scared." Tony crossed back to the mixer to check on the dough.

"But—but Phil Sidler is dead. What is she afraid of now?" Joe drummed his fingers on a countertop. "Where was she going when she left here?" he asked.

"Don't know." Tony raised his voice to be heard over the whir of the machine. "I guess she went back to where she's staying. She asked for her pay this morning and quit her job—"

"Let's go, Frank," Joe said, cutting off Tony.

They dashed to the van and took off for Annie's apartment. "Let me see Annie alone, Frank?" Joe asked as Frank snugged up to the curb.

"Sorry, pal. I'm going in with you." Frank thought of Phil's room, and he had a bad feeling about this one.

Joe shrugged and bolted. Frank followed as soon as he had pocketed the keys.

Inside, the old apartment building was even worse than it looked on the outside. The stairway was dark—all the bulbs were broken or burned out. The institutional green paint was peeling, and the combined odors of stale cooking grease and damp turned the boys' stomachs.

Joe referred to the row of mailboxes in the entryway before taking the stairs two at a time to the third floor. The creak of each step accented the soft thud of Joe's sneakers hitting the treads.

Right behind him, Frank snatched at Joe's arm when they reached the third floor. "Joe, wait. Whoever searched Phil's apartment may have done the same to Annie's. Or maybe he's doing it now. If we go busting in there—"

Joe shrugged off Frank's grasp. "You're right. If they've hurt Annie, I'll . . ." Clenching his teeth, Joe forced himself to slow down. The boys crept slowly along, looking in both directions.

The door to the first apartment in the third-floor hall was ajar. Joe glanced in. A small child with huge brown eyes peered up at him. Frank stepped around to see what Joe was looking at. He smiled.

"Cammie, shut that door and get in here," a shrill voice sounded. But the child only stuck her thumb in her mouth and continued to stare at Frank, who waved.

He moved back to glance over the banister, viewing the entire stairway. They'd seen no one but the child, and everything seemed normal enough. Somewhere, the muffled sound of a blaring television set spewed out a game show, the announcer's voice probably describing dozens of wonderful prizes.

Joe pointed to the last door in the hallway. Quietly they made their way down to it. Each took a position on either side of the door. Joe started to knock, but at his touch the door creaked open.

"Annie? What—" Joe called out. He pushed the door back and stepped into the room, Frank acting as his shadow.

The room was in the same condition as the one in the Bayport Downtowner. Chairs were overturned, the upholstery ripped open, dirty cotton stuffing was strewn beside them, looking like the spilled guts from a corpse. One wall of the room had been turned into a makeshift kitchen; pots and pans now spilled out in front of it.

Almost soundlessly Joe headed for a room off to the left. He swung the door open.

The bedroom was in a similar state. Blankets had been tossed to the floor in a heap. The mattress had been slashed and gutted like the chairs. Drawers were piled on the floor, their contents dumped out. Annie's clothing had been tossed everywhere. A red sweater hung limply from the mirror like a flag on a windless day.

Joe, out of patience and no longer cautious, shouted out frantically. "Annie! You here?" He pushed open the door to the tiny bathroom and glanced at the tub. He was almost afraid to look.

No one. It was empty. What Joe feared most had happened. Annie was gone!

Chapter
6

"WHERE IS SHE?" Joe groaned and leaned against the bathroom doorframe.

Frank could hear the pain in his brother's voice, but there was little he could do to comfort him. "I don't know, Joe, but when I went to take a look at Sidler's room in the Bayport Downtowner, it looked just like this."

"Why didn't you tell me last night?" Joe asked. "You knew Annie was in danger. We could have come and gotten her."

"I wasn't thinking straight, Joe. Sorry, but I guess I thought she'd be fine." Frank leaned in to touch his brother's arm. "Joe—"

"Leave me alone." Joe knocked Frank's hand away.

"Joe, Annie may have left town. She may have

run away. She drew her pay, quit her job. That means she must have had a plan."

"She wouldn't have left town without telling me, Frank." Joe's voice pleaded that she hadn't. "I know she wouldn't."

"Let's search the building." Frank gave Joe new hope.

"I know she said there's storage in the basement. She put her suitcases down there. But she would have to take them if she'd left." With restored purpose, Joe took off into the hall and down the stairs to check out the basement.

Frank took the time to stop at the open door they'd passed. He knocked and looked down at the child, who smiled up at him.

"Cammie— Who?" A tired-looking woman snatched up her child. "Who are you? Get out of here."

"Sorry, ma'am. The door was open. I wanted to ask if you heard anything unusual last night or this morning. Or if you've seen the red-haired woman who lives on this floor."

"I didn't hear anything. I didn't see anything, or anyone, either. We mind our own business here. Now, get out."

Frank backed away from the door and left the woman scolding her daughter for opening it in the first place. Bounding down the stairs, he caught up with Joe, who had just checked out the first floor.

"The basement's this way," Joe said, leading Frank to a door at the end of the hall.

The light Joe flicked on at the top of the stairs didn't help much. The stairwell was dim, and the stairs were dusty. If anyone in the building was in charge of maintenance, he or she took the job lightly. Frank stepped in front of Joe and started down slowly, one step at a time.

Frank doubted that whoever searched Annie's room would think to check the storage area, but it paid to proceed cautiously. He knew that Joe wanted to throw caution aside and burst into the basement.

The basement was empty. Joe's face was grim. "I think that's probably a storage room over there," he said loudly, his voice bouncing off the concrete walls.

Just as they reached the storage room and were inspecting the padlock on the door, they were surprised by a voice behind them. "Joe?" The whisper seemed like a shout in the cool quiet.

"Annie!" Joe turned and ran to her as she stepped out of a nearby closet. He caught her just as she started to collapse.

"Joe, I was so afraid I'd never see you again," Annie said faintly.

"You know better than that. I'm just glad I thought about the basement. What are you doing here?"

"Hoping you'd find me!" Annie burst into tears.

Joe reassured Annie that he was there to help her.

Frank sighed. Although glad Annie had been found, he couldn't help wishing they could put her on a bus with a ticket to someplace far away. Whatever trouble Annie had gotten herself into now directly involved Joe.

"What happened, Annie?" Frank asked, questioning the girl. "Who searched your room?"

"I don't know, Frank." Annie stepped from the safety of Joe's arms. She blew her nose on a tissue Joe provided. The tears on her face streaked the dirt and dust she had collected in her hiding place, and even Frank felt protective. She looked as vulnerable as a young child.

"I came back from Tony's this morning," Annie continued, "and walked in on a guy trashing my room. I'd never seen him before, but obviously he'd been there for a while. Obviously you saw it." Annie choked back another sob. "Joe, he tried to kill me! I ran. I've been here, hiding, ever since."

"He tried to kill you?" Frank questioned. "Did he have a gun—a knife? What did he look like? Can you describe him?"

"It all happened so fast. I—I don't know."

"Someone searched your room and threatened

to kill you, Annie. You must remember something. Think. Did he have a gun?"

"No." Annie threw a glance at Joe that seemed to say, "Make your brother leave me alone." She was sending out a signal loud and clear—damsel in distress, damsel in distress.

"Frank, cool it. You don't have to come on like a tough cop. Annie's had a bad scare. Let's go so she can clean up. We'll get a soda and talk like civilized people."

Frank ignored Joe. "We'll get out of here in a minute. Annie, did he pull a knife on you?" He returned his attention to the girl.

"I—I don't think so."

"How did he try to kill you? Did he grab you, try to strangle you?" Frank asked.

"Frank, I was scared." Annie was getting angry at him and his tone of voice. "I— Maybe he didn't try to kill me, but I thought he was going to. He pushed me aside and ran when I walked in on him."

"Now we're getting somewhere," Frank said, glancing at Joe. "What did the man look like, Annie?"

"I don't know. He—he was tall. Really tall."

And quick, Frank added to himself. That is, if it was the same guy who startled him in Phil's room. It wasn't much to go on, but it was something. Whoever had been looking for Phil obviously knew that Annie had some connection to him.

At this point, though, there was only one thing that Frank was perfectly certain of. Whatever was going on, Annie *was* scared. Frank had seen pure fear before, and recognized it now in the girl's eyes. Maybe he had been too hard on her with his questions. After all, he hadn't noticed anything when he was surprised by what seemed to be the same attacker. Anyway, no matter how much he wished Joe wasn't involved with her— he was. And now, so was Frank. They had to help her.

"Annie, I think you should know that the police suspect that Phil Sidler was a thief." Frank realized he might be telling Annie something she already knew. "In fact, he's been connected to a gang of jewel thieves that has been active in the New York area for some time. Now, we think that because you knew Phil, and someone knows you knew him, you may be in very real danger."

"What should I do, Frank?" Annie clung to Joe's hand. "I'm scared to death." She turned wide eyes on Frank. "You'll help me, won't you?" She looked lost and childlike.

"You know we will, Annie."

"I don't know anything about Phil Sidler," Annie said. "I mean, not recently."

"When was the last time you saw him?" Joe

asked. Frank was glad to hear Joe switch to a more businesslike tone.

"I—I can't remember." Annie frowned. "I did visit his mother before I came to Bayport. That would have been, let's see, just over a month ago."

"When had his mother last seen him?" Frank asked as he led the way back upstairs to Annie's apartment.

"She said she hadn't seen him in a long time, but she made me read a letter that Phil had written to her." Annie paused as if wondering whether or not to go on. "She—well, she always wanted Phil and me to stay together. She was urging me to go find Phil."

"Did you look at the address on the letter? Where was Phil when he wrote it?" Frank continued to press for information.

"I glanced at it, since his mother kept insisting I look at it. I think it was a Hundred-eleventh or -twelfth Street, something like that. In New York City."

"It's not much to go on. But I found a matchbook cover outside Phil's apartment. It came from a bar on Amsterdam Avenue, way uptown. I think I'm going to take a little trip to the city. And I think, Annie, that I'd better share with you all the information I have so far."

"I'm going, too, Frank," Joe answered. "Anything we find out will help Annie. Obviously someone thinks she knows something, and she's involved whether she wants to be or not."

"I'm not staying here alone," Annie protested. "I'll go also. Besides," she added shyly, with a hint of the old sparkle in her eyes, "you know I always wanted to watch you detectives in action."

"Okay," Joe agreed. "Get your stuff ready. I'll run down for your suitcases. You're not staying here anymore."

They waited until Annie washed up, changed into a skirt and heels, and threw her stuff into the bags, which they tossed in the back of the van. After pulling into a fast-food place, they ordered hamburgers, fries, and sodas, which they ate on the way to the city.

The trio sat quietly as Frank maneuvered through the traffic on the streets of the Upper West Side of Manhattan.

Finding the bar was easy, and Frank luckily got a parking spot nearby. It was nearly five o'clock, the time the bar started to fill with customers. It was small and shabby, and the bartender was especially friendly.

"Hiya, folks. Welcome to Norm's. Long time no see, A—"

"Are you Norm?" Annie cut off the greeting and laughed. "Sorry to bother you, Norm, but we just need some information. My friends are looking for a guy named Phil Sidler. Lived around here, we think.''

None of Annie's earlier fear showed in this exchange. She stepped easily into the role of private investigator. She seemed to have a natural talent for the work. ''Tall, blond, wore his hair in long sideburns. Big nose, so thin if he turned sideways you might miss him,'' she joked.

The bartender grinned, eyeing Annie curiously. ''Good description. What's this information worth to you?''

Annie dug in her purse and pulled out a twenty. She casually tucked it into the glass closest to her as she perched on a bar stool.

''Last time I saw him, he called the Riverview Apartments home.'' Norm continued to arrange beer mugs in neat rows, all the time keeping a cheerful smile on his face. ''Two blocks west of here, on a Hundred and twelfth.''

''Thanks, Norm—if you're Norm.'' Annie smiled and rejoined the Hardys, who had watched the exchange with astonishment. ''Not bad, huh?'' she whispered to Joe.

''You're hired,'' said Joe, putting his arm around Annie and escorting her out onto the street. ''Our agency could use a woman.'' He grinned at Annie as if the two of them were alone, and Annie looked relieved that she had done well in spite of her nervousness.

Meanwhile, Frank was deep in thought. Had

he imagined it, or had the bartender recognized Annie as they entered the bar? He glanced at the smiling, wholesome-looking girl, beaming under Joe's affectionate praise. Surely Frank was wrong. Why would a nice nineteen-year-old girl be known in a dive like that?

Frank erased the thought from his mind. He had too many other things to worry about now.

Even though the Riverview Apartments were just two blocks from Norm's bar, they moved the van and parked beside the curb outside the red-brick building. If there was any view of the river from the building, it would be from the roof, Frank thought, on a clear day. They approached the entrance but stopped at the bottom of the three steps.

"How do we get in?" Joe looked at the wrought-iron gate in front of the entrance door. Each needed a key.

"Up to you, Annie." Frank and Joe quickly disappeared around the corner to watch Annie.

She waited a couple of minutes, until an overweight, matronly woman started toward the building, then she took a deep breath and stepped into the role as if she were made for it. Quickly Annie rummaged through her purse. "I've done it again," she said, scolding herself as the woman approached the door of the building. "Phil will kill me if I've lost it."

"Left your key inside, did you?" The woman

asked, eyeing Annie suspiciously. "You young people are so careless these days."

"Oh, thank goodness." Annie looked at the woman with relief, ignoring her doubtful gaze. "At least I can wait for Phil in the hall instead of on the doorstep." She chattered on, charming the woman, and finally entered the building with her. Annie even held her groceries while she opened the two doors into the Riverview Apartments.

"Pretty good member of our team, huh, Frank?" Joe said as the Hardys approached the door moments later. Annie held the front door open, and they slipped through.

"Apartment Seventeen, top floor," Annie whispered. "His name is still on the box."

The Hardys, trusting Annie's skills by now, pushed the button for the small, rickety elevator and rode up in silence.

"Oh!" Annie stepped backward right into Joe and gasped as the door to 17 swung open. It was not locked. Inside, the picture was the same—someone had been there, too.

They made a quick search, but expected to find nothing. Annie stood in the middle of the one tiny dark room the whole time, glancing over her shoulder and twisting the ring on her finger nervously.

"Let's get out of here, guys. I don't like this." After seeing this new evidence, Annie was no longer pleased to be playing detective.

Frank didn't like it, either, but he wanted to search thoroughly, anyway. He didn't know what he expected to find.

Once again there was nothing. Whoever was employed in the search-and-destroy division of this operation was skilled and thorough.

"Okay, let's go," he said, and led the way back to the elevator.

Out on the sidewalk in front of the building, they all gratefully breathed in the fresh air. Annie walked toward the van ahead of the brothers, anxious to be safe inside the vehicle. As she was passing a limousine parked at the curb, both passenger doors opened.

Before either of the Hardys could react, two men dressed entirely in black leaped out and grabbed Annie, who barely had time to let out one short scream.

The men wrestled Annie into the car and roared away.

Chapter

7

"No!" SHOUTED JOE.

"Let's go after them," Frank yelled, heading for the van. "Keep your eye on that car."

The Hardys dashed for their van, and Frank had the engine roaring before Joe fastened his seat belt.

Frank followed the limo easily, racing through yellow lights and weaving in and out of traffic. But near a group of warehouses a red light stopped them. Frank had been so intent on chasing the limo that he didn't notice it until it was too late. It was then that he heard the scream of a siren and saw a red flashing light appear in his rearview mirror.

"Ignore them," Joe urged. "We'll lose Annie." He sat forward in his seat as if he could help Frank drive faster.

Frank heaved a sigh. "I can't, Joe. Keep an eye on the limo as long as possible." Frank pulled the van to the curb and waited for the ticket that was certain to follow.

When Frank stopped, Joe jerked open his door and hit the sidewalk running. One of the police officers called out to him, but he ignored the man's shouts. He sprinted after the limo for two blocks, watching it pull farther and farther away. Annie, he thought determinedly, I can't lose you now.

The black car slowed at an intersection, and just as Joe thought he might catch up, it turned right and disappeared. Joe pounded the concrete even harder until he reached the corner where the limo had turned. There was an empty lot on one side, an old building surrounded by a high fence on the other, and directly in front of him a ramp that led to underground parking.

Joe's lungs burned as his breath came in ragged spurts, and his legs, with the oxygen depleted, felt heavy as lead. He glanced around, knowing the limo hadn't gone farther. It had to have gone down the ramp.

Cautiously he slipped into the cool darkness that led under a building. The light was dim, but as soon as Joe's eyes adjusted, he saw only a few cars in a neat row. Was the building abandoned?

No black limo. This was impossible. The limo couldn't just vanish.

"Okay," snapped the officer, with his hand ready on the butt of his gun as Frank rolled down the window. "Out of the van—with your hands up. Let's hear your excuse for running a red light, and in your pal's case, escaping to avoid arrest."

"Officer, I know this is going to sound wild . . ." Frank began, obediently climbing out of the car. Obviously, Joe's running off had alerted the cops to trouble. The officer's partner stood on the passenger side of the van—his hand also ready to draw his revolver—speaking into a two-way radio.

"We're chasing a black limousine. Two guys jumped out and kidnapped a friend of ours." Frank tried to sound convincing. "A girl. Please believe me. This is urgent."

The officer grinned. "Well, I haven't heard *that* story before. Good, kid, real good. Let's see your license. Officer Nolan, check the registration," he added to his partner. "Is it in the glove compartment?" he asked.

Frank nodded and handed his license over. "I swear it's true, sir," he continued. "Can you just check it out? Then I'll take the ticket. The van is mine."

"In a minute, kid. Before I do anything I'm

going to search the van—with your permission, of course—for any illegal substances.''

"Papers check out, Officer Delgado," Nolan said. "I'm going after his buddy. He must have had some reason to run." He took off in the direction that Joe had run.

"Check out the black limo while you're at it, Nolan," Delgado called sarcastically. "I'll keep an eye on this one."

"Will do," Officer Nolan called back.

Delgado checked out the van and then took Frank's license and walked slowly back to the patrol car with it.

Frank climbed back in the van and pounded the door once, letting out his frustration. It took way too long to write a ticket, he thought, looking for Joe or Nolan.

Finally Officer Delgado returned. "Your license is good and no tickets lately." The man seemed surprised, as if he had expected Frank to have a record. "Sign here." He shoved a clipboard through Frank's window along with a ballpoint pen.

Frank looked it over. This was going to cost him, and his dad would be furious, but even worse was not knowing where Joe was. He scribbled his name and handed back the clipboard.

"Your father's Fenton Hardy?" the officer asked.

"Yes, sir," Frank said with no further comment. His dad was a former New York City detective, but Frank would never have mentioned his father's name or connections under these circumstances.

"He's not going to like this, I'd guess."

"No, sir. May I go now?" Frank was poised, ready to turn the key in the ignition.

"Let's see what my partner and your friend found." Delgado pointed out Nolan and Joe, who were just returning.

Nolan caught Delgado's eye and shook his head a couple of times. Joe, who was staring straight ahead, had a disgusted look on his face.

Delgado grinned. "Black limo? Life-or-death matter? Good try, Hardy," he said, and patted Frank's door once. "You're free, kid."

Frank turned then to Joe, who'd crawled into the passenger seat. "Did you lose it?"

"The limo turned right and vanished, Frank." Joe bit his lip, looking grim.

"Vanished? You sure?"

"Sure I'm sure. It wasn't that far ahead of me. There's an empty lot on one side, a fence around an old building on the other. I checked every car in this underground lot that it had to have turned into. Nothing."

"Let's check it out again." Frank drove the two blocks.

The underground lot was posted PRIVATE, NO

PARKING, VIOLATORS WILL BE TOWED. Frank pulled onto the ramp despite the warnings. He wanted to see for himself.

"Let's look around again, Joe. It's our only lead. We can't give up."

"I'm not giving up," Joe said. "A car that big doesn't just disappear."

"It could have taken off by now," Frank said, calmly assessing the situation.

Either that or the black limo *had* disappeared into thin air. There was no clue of any kind. The boys even checked the walls for a button to a hidden panel, but they found nothing.

After driving back up the ramp, the Hardys carefully searched the area within a two-block radius. Nothing. Feeling dejected, they headed back to the underground parking lot and down the ramp. One more look-see, they decided.

They'd lost Annie to who knows who or what. They hopped out their doors—neither wanted to give up. Joe walked around the front of the van to join his brother.

"When are you going to call it quits, boys?" a man said, moving up on them from the rear of the van.

The Hardys spun around to face two men all in black. They wore black ski masks over their faces with only their eyes and mouths showing. But it wasn't the men's appearances that held the Hardys' attention.

It was the pair of Browning 9mm automatic pistols that they had aimed at the brothers' hearts.

Chapter

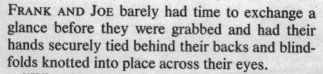

8

FRANK AND JOE barely had time to exchange a glance before they were grabbed and had their hands securely tied behind their backs and blindfolds knotted into place across their eyes.

"What have you done with Annie?" Joe demanded. He and Frank stumbled as they were prodded to move blindly forward.

"Ain't that sweet, Clive? The kid's worried about his girlfriend."

"If you've hurt her . . ." Joe's threat died out as he realized there was nothing he could do at the moment.

"What'll you do about it? You gonna be a hero?" The thug laughed. "We got us a Prince Charming, Clive."

"Shut up, Hodge. Just move along."

Frank was trying to memorize by smell and sound where they were being taken. They didn't walk far before they entered an elevator. A strong chemical smell, not unlike that of shoe polish, permeated the space.

The smell disappeared the minute they left the elevator. There was a deep carpet underfoot now, and they were being led down what seemed to be a long hall.

"Good evening, boys," a voice greeted them just before their blindfolds were removed. "I'm sorry to inconvenience you, but you'll soon appreciate the reason for this secrecy."

Frank blinked twice to focus his eyes. Then he looked around, amazed. The men who had grabbed them were now wearing mirrored sunglasses instead of their ski masks.

The office they were in was decorated only in black and white. Walls were stark white, broken up randomly by a series of black and white abstract paintings. The carpet at their feet, deep and luxurious, was slightly off-white. The desktop in front of them looked as if it were fashioned from one solid piece of pure black marble.

And behind the desk, leaning back casually in a large office chair, sat a tall man. His long legs were crossed at the ankles and were resting on the marble top as if he were attending a casual meeting. He wore a finely tailored black business suit. His hair had been recently styled, but the boys couldn't see his eyes; they were hidden behind mirrored sunglasses.

And he wore diamonds. Many diamonds. On his right pinkie finger, on top of a thin, white leather glove, he sported an enormous, many-faceted diamond ring. A small diamond sparkled in the lobe of one of his ears. And the finishing touch was a diamond stickpin pushed jauntily into his black tie. Frank was no expert, but it hardly took a jeweler to appraise the stone in that ring. If the diamond was real, it had to be worth at least a million.

The man's tone as he greeted them was that of a polite host at a party. He smiled. But his smile was as cold and hard as the diamond in his tie. And his gloved hands he kept to himself, the fingers interlocked and resting on his out-stretched legs.

"Who are you?" asked Joe, shrugging off the hands that still held him. "Where's Annie?"

"I'm right here, Joe." Annie's voice came from behind them as a third man pushed her forward.

"Are you all right, Annie?" Joe started to move to her, but strong hands kept him where he was.

"I—I guess so," Annie stammered.

On the desk in front of the head man, Frank recognized the black purse that Annie had kept clutched to her. Its contents were spilled out

across a white blotter. Frank's quick eye inven-
toried the contents, and he was surprised to find
that Annie had been hiding a secret.

She was in possession of a gun. Why would a
girl who was a waitress in a pizza joint need to be
armed?

"What do you want with us?" Joe asked, growing more impatient.

The man smiled again, perfect white teeth glit-
tering in his wide mouth. "Forgive me for not
making the introductions. My name is Cutter,
Mr. Cutter. You are Frank and Joe Hardy, are
you not?"

"How do you know that?" Joe asked.

Cutter chuckled. "I don't bring in visitors without knowing their identities."

"Do you always tie up and blindfold your
guests?" asked Frank, trying to decide how much
danger they were in.

"Untie them," Cutter commanded, gracefully
lowering his legs to the floor. "It was merely a
precaution. But on to the business at hand." He
pushed the contents of Annie's purse—minus the
gun—back into the bag. Annie stepped forward
to claim it, anger in her movements.

The man slowly smiled at her. And then he
quickly relaxed the gesture of friendliness and
tightened his lips into a straight line. "Where are
the diamonds, Annie? Phil double-crossed me,
but I know you can't be that foolish."

Frank and Joe stared at the tall red-haired girl beside them, waiting for her answer.

"I don't know what you're talking about," she protested. "I've told you . . ."

"You were good friends with Phil Sidler—"

Annie cut him off. "A while ago. I'm not responsible for what he was involved in now. So bringing me here is a waste of time."

Frank couldn't tell if Annie was bluffing or not. But he had spent enough time with her that day to know that she was a fairly competent actress. Was she acting now?

Cutter sat forward, his impatience growing. "So far, I have treated you as my guest, Annie, you and your friends here. I'm a patient man, but I have been known to lose my patience. At which point I have ways of getting the information I need."

"She told you she knew nothing," said Joe, stepping toward Cutter's desk.

At Cutter's signal, the three henchmen moved forward to take Annie's, Frank's, and Joe's arms once again. "You impress me as intelligent young people—if a bit reckless. In my experience, young people never have all the money they'd like. I'm in a very lucrative business, and good help is hard to find. I'll tell you what I'm going to do."

He paused for effect, looking at each of his prisoners. "I can guarantee you each a more-than-generous salary, and a bonus for each job well done. I would, of course, expect Annie to return the items in her possession that belong to me. This would indicate her willingness to join me. I'll give you time to think over my offer." Cutter stood up then and indicated with a turn of his head that Joe, Frank, and Annie were to be escorted from his office.

The gun between Frank's shoulder blades kept him from protesting or trying to get away. The trio was led down a hall and shoved into another room. The lock clicked behind them.

The room was a small gym, fitted with weight machines, a stationary bike, a rowing machine, and mirrors.

Frank looked around. "Nothing like the Y, is it?" he said, making an attempt at humor. "Listen, Annie, whatever you're mixed up in, it's time to level with us. Obviously we're on the same side for the moment." He gave her a searching look. When she didn't answer, he said, "I think you'd better start by explaining why you were carrying a gun."

"Wouldn't you—if you were me?" Annie exploded angrily. Then she reined in her fury. "I was scared," she said. "When that man attacked me in my own apartment—of course I wanted to defend myself." Her hazel eyes pleaded with Frank to understand. "The gun is my father's," she said. "I took it when I left home. He was—

well, he was pretty abusive, and I was afraid he might go crazy and come after me with it when he found out I was gone. I decided to keep it when I got to Bayport—just in case. I was on my own, after all."

She glanced at Joe, whose level gaze had never left her. "I never would have used it," she said weakly, trying to smile at him.

"What about you and Phil?" Frank demanded.

Annie released a deep breath. "I'll tell you the same thing I told Cutter. I have no idea what Phil Sidler was involved in now. My bad luck was that I cared for him. I met him when I was in high school. I was just a kid."

It wasn't as if Annie was an old lady now. Frank wasn't sure he believed her, but he had no choice but to let the matter drop.

"Okay, here's the way I figure it." He leaned back against the saddle of the bicycle. "Cutter's behind all the jewel robberies in the area for the last several months, maybe longer. Obviously he specializes in diamonds. Phil Sidler double-crossed him, and because Phil contacted Annie, Cutter now thinks Annie has the diamonds or knows where they are." Frank held up a hand, palm out, to stop Annie from protesting again.

"He thinks cutting us in is the easiest way to get the diamonds back," added Joe, relieved that Frank wasn't dumping on Annie anymore. "Right now we've got two choices. We can pretend to join them. Or we can try to get out of here."

Frank looked around. There were no windows; it looked as if the door they came in was the only way back out.

"Would you trust Cutter?" asked Annie. "I don't think he'd cut us in on his business."

"I didn't say we'd trust him. Only pretend to join him." Frank checked each piece of equipment. "Do you think he was the guy in your apartment, Annie?"

"I don't know. But I think I'd have remembered the way he was dressed."

"He might wear civvies when he's out of here," Joe said, looking around at the well-appointed gym. Unable to resist, he jabbed at a punching bag hanging from the ceiling in a corner of the room.

"Annie, I can't blame you for not being able to describe the man in your room," Frank said. "I only got a glimpse of the guy who stunned me at Phil's. But he was tall, and quick. Like he worked out every day. I think it could have been Cutter."

"If Cutter has all these thugs working for him, Frank, it makes more sense for him to send them to do his dirty work," Joe argued logically.

"You're right." Frank silently ran through their options. "I don't think we can pretend to go along with Cutter's offer. I think we'd better try to break out. I just don't trust him. I think we'll do better taking action on our own."

"I agree." Joe looked around. "This should do the job." He lifted the dumbbell from the bench press after removing several weights. "Not that I can't lift that much." Joe grinned at Annie. "But it's unwieldy when it's that heavy. This should be just about right." He tossed the bell slightly.

Frank was catching on to Joe's plan. "Wonder how long they'll leave us here? We could get a pretty good workout. I've been short of time lately." He sat down, adjusted the cable beside him, and pushed the hand grips of the weight machine forward, pressing fifty pounds.

"You admit you're turning into a ninety-eight-pound weakling?" Joe kidded.

"How can you two mess around at a time like this?" Annie complained. "These guys'll kill us if we don't cooperate." She slumped down on the floor beside the rowing machine.

"They could," Joe agreed, walking close to the door with the dumbbell.

"They won't kill you, Annie. They think you have some information they need. But you might wish they would kill you." Frank joined Joe at the door.

"Leave her alone, Frank," Joe said to his brother. "We need to concentrate on getting out of here. Call them, Annie. I'm tired of waiting."

Annie went over to the door and leaned her ear

against it. Then she knocked. "You win, guys," she said into the crack where the door met the frame. "I'll tell you everything."

No answer. It seemed as though there was no one outside the door. But a click signaled that someone *had* been waiting for Annie's reply. The door was swung open slowly, and a gun was thrust into the room.

"Okay, come on out. It didn't take you long to make up your minds." Cutter grinned, and Frank, right behind Annie, could see her mirrored in his sunglasses.

Frank then went into action. In a single motion he shoved Annie past Cutter with his left hand, and with his right delivered a single karate chop to the man's gun hand. Joe was right behind him.

"Here, catch," said Joe, tossing the dumbbell to the second man.

The thug's automatic reaction was to raise his hands to deflect the weight. As he did so, Joe grabbed his gun arm, twisting it so that he released the Browning as the dumbbell fell to the floor. Before the two knew what had hit them, they had been disarmed and locked into their own prison.

"At least they'll have something to do," Joe quipped. "I thought they were grossly out of condition, didn't you, Frank?"

The hall ran both ways, but instinct sent the boys in the direction from which they'd come.

The carpet muffled their footsteps as they hurried to the elevator. Inside the huge cage, the three stood silently gritting their teeth, their patience stretched thin by the slowness of the descent.

The door opened into the parking garage, and the trio started to dash out, Joe's hand around Annie's arm.

They stopped abruptly. Frank knew right then—without a doubt—that the tall man who'd knocked him out at Phil's was not Cutter.

Because here, blocking the entrance to the elevator, had to be his playmate from the hotel. This man was six-six, at least. As Frank watched, the tall man grabbed both Annie and Joe. He raised a revolver and held it steady. It was pointed straight at Annie's head.

Chapter

9

"ALL RIGHT, KIDS," the man said coolly. "It's time for some answers. We'll talk in your van. Move." He pointed the way with his gun, and when they didn't move fast enough, he nudged Joe forward by ramming the barrel into his spine.

"Ahhh!" Joe's breath rushed out in one burst, and he fell forward from the waist. Frank whirled around, his hands raised, ready to strike. But the tall man was too fast for him and kept his gun level and trained on both Frank and Joe.

Annie took a step back out of the man's line of sight. Before Joe could say, "Make your move, Annie," she had done so. Pulling her arm back to maximum power, Annie smashed the tall man just behind the ear with the heel of her hand. He was out cold.

Frank and Joe must have been wearing identical looks of astonishment, because Annie answered their question before it was asked. "I learned karate in junior high. I was a brown belt when I was fifteen."

"Good work," Frank said, meaning it.

"We're out of here!" Joe said, and reached out for Annie's arm. It was an unnecessary action, since she was ready to move before he was.

In the van, with the engine roaring, Joe advised Frank to head for home. "We need someplace to plan our next move and hide Annie."

"I think it's obvious that a lot of people know who we are. So they probably know where we live. I don't think we should go home; we'll only put Mom and Aunt Gertrude in danger."

"Do you have a better idea?" Joe snapped. "We've got to find someplace safe for Annie."

"I don't want to put your family in danger," she said defensively. "Frank thinks I've put them in enough already. If you'll drop me at the bus station in Bayport, I can disappear on my own."

"No way," Joe said, throwing Frank an annoyed glance. "I can't do that. We'll hide you someplace. Don't worry. If you aren't involved, you'll be free to live anyplace you like."

Frank noticed that Joe had said "if." Had he done some thinking about Annie? One thing was clear to anyone: she had gotten rid of the tall man unbelievably fast and efficiently. Also, she didn't seem to be as frightened as she had been earlier. Frank wondered why she had ever felt scared at all with a gun in her purse and a karate chop like the one she used on the tall man.

Frank changed his mind and headed for home.

After Frank discussed the case with his father, Fenton Hardy was of two opinions. Yes, he thought it was risky business bringing Annie into the Hardy home. But he agreed with Joe that it was more risky to leave her out on the street alone.

"Even though Joe is only in this mess because of her, Frank," Mr. Hardy said, "we are involved. *And* she is the key witness to Joe's accident."

Frank moved on to another subject. "Do you have any ideas about who this mysterious Cutter might be?"

"Just waiting for you to ask." Fenton Hardy got up and went to his file cabinet and flipped through several drawers as he went back half a dozen years. "Here it is."

"You know him?" Frank asked excitedly.

"Daniel Cutter was a small-time safecracker until he proved that he could open any safe. His reputation grew. The Cutter, they started to call him. Everyone wanted him to work for them. But he got careless or ran out of luck about ten years ago. A gas tank from an acetylene torch exploded in his face.''

"The glasses . . ." Frank mused. "And the gloves. It must be the same guy. But he's working on a new nickname now. He's into jewelry heists. Diamond Dan Cutter would suit him. I estimated he was wearing over a million dollars' worth of stones.''

Fenton Hardy nodded distractedly, his mind obviously moving in new directions. "Maybe he didn't really know who you were even though he knew your names. You were only Annie's companions to him." Fenton Hardy closed the file drawer and wandered back to his desk. "It's impossible to trace diamonds after they've been cut, recut, or reset. Our only hope is if you can take us back to the gang's hideout.''

"Finding the building is a snap, but I don't know the secret to get up to the apartment. I know you don't just get on the elevator.''

"Sorry, Frank, but I don't like it. I'm going to have to turn all this information over to the police. I don't want you to go back there alone. Okay?''

Frank met his father's eyes and slowly nodded. "Okay. I agree. I'm going to talk to Joe now.''

"Tell him the police want to see him in the morning. The more he cooperates, the better it looks. I don't want him doing anything reckless. You and Annie can go with him. They might want to ask you some more questions after I speak with them."

"Sure, Dad." Frank headed for the kitchen, the first place in the Hardy house to look for Joe.

Joe had helped Annie get settled in the guest room and then gone back to the kitchen to polish off the food they'd picked up at a deli. He sat at the kitchen table, drinking a glass of milk and eating a ham and swiss on rye.

"Joe, I've done some thinking." Frank pulled out a pad of paper from behind the kitchen phone. "Look at this."

Joe was interested in Frank's time schedule until he found out that all the events involved only Annie.

"Annie gets the phone call from Phil, which we witnessed," Frank said, beginning his list of facts. "According to her, that was the first time she'd heard from Phil in ages. Right?"

"What are you getting at, Frank?"

"Hold on. Try to think for a minute, and don't just act on your feelings for Annie." Frank sat down beside Joe.

Joe grumbled but kept listening.

"The next several hours we all spent at the police station. I took Annie home, but we know she spent that night at Mr. Pizza in the store-room, right?"

"What are you getting at?" Joe asked again.

"Either she got the gun out of storage after she was attacked, as she said, or she could have had it in her purse all along—before Phil called her on the phone." Frank stared at his brother but Joe only looked at the last of his sandwich. Frank continued.

"I think that Annie already had the gun, Joe, that she'd seen Phil or heard from him before that phone call. We know he checked in at the hotel two days earlier. Now, she was scared of someone—even after Phil was dead. That was why she spent the night at Mr. Pizza." He took a deep breath. "I think that someone was Cutter and his men. She knew he'd be looking for her."

"I don't want to hear any more of these crazy ideas, Frank." Joe stood up.

"I'm afraid my 'crazy ideas' are right on target this time. Or if not, you tell me why *both* Cutter and the tall man think Annie has the diamonds. Doesn't that strike you as strange, Joe? Face it, Annie isn't telling us the whole story. She's not only a girl dealing with a jealous boyfriend, she's a stranger with a gun and a mean karate chop—"

"If you're trying to convince me Annie's a jewel thief, forget it. I admit that everything doesn't fall into place, but Annie Shea is not a crook."

"You're not thinking, Joe."

"Yes. I am. And what's more, I've decided

80

that Annie isn't staying in Bayport a minute longer. I'm going to take her someplace safe.''

"Where? Dad wants us all to go down to the Bayport police station tomorrow, to tell them about everything that's happened. They specifically want to see you at ten o'clock. And then we'll probably have to talk to New York cops— since we were taken by Cutter and his goons there.''

"I'm taking Annie upstate, Frank. That's it. Once I get her safely hidden away, I can work on the case and talk to the police.''

"Joe, not being available to the police tomorrow morning is like admitting you're guilty. They'll think you skipped out on your bail. Dad could get in big trouble, too.''

"Hold on, Frank.'' Joe started to move to the kitchen door. "I'll be back before they know I'm gone.''

"I'm not going to let you go, Joe.'' Frank stepped in front of his brother.

Joe laughed. "You're not going to *let* me go? Out of my way, Frank. Please, get out of my way.''

Frank faced him and realized what he knew all along—it would be impossible to stop his brother once he made up his mind to go.

"If you screw up, Joe, don't expect me to cover for you,'' Frank said to his back.

"I won't, Frank. I promise. And I *will* be back on time." Joe patted his brother on the shoulder and took off.

Frank banged his fist on the counter in frustration as Joe Hardy disappeared up the stairs.

Chapter

10

JOE KNOCKED AT Annie's door. "Annie, you asleep?"

"No, Joe. Come on in. What's wrong?" Annie sat on the side of her bed, still dressed, her suitcases unopened. "I've been trying to figure out what to do. I've already caused too much trouble."

"I have a plan, Annie. I'm glad you haven't unpacked anything. We're leaving here."

"Where are we going?" Annie stood up and slipped on her shoes.

"I have a friend who has a cabin upstate. There are a couple of small motels in the area. I'm going to take you up there and hide you out in a motel until this mess gets worked out. Then I'll come back for you."

Annie stared at Joe. "Joe, I told you I'll just leave town, disappear."

"No, Annie. Trust me. If you lay low for a few days, I can crack this case. But I can't if I'm worrying about you."

"I can take care of myself," said Annie.

"I did notice that," Joe said with admiration in his voice. "But something might come up that even you can't handle."

Annie's eyes held his for a moment and she said nothing. "This is Frank's idea, isn't it?" she said finally. "To get me away from you."

"Frank wants you to stay," Joe insisted. "He's—he's concerned about you."

Annie laughed bitterly. "He's never liked me," she said. "Maybe it's because I'm not like Callie. I don't have parents who take care of me and have money and—"

"Annie," Joe interrupted, taking her hand. "Who cares what Frank thinks? I like you—a lot. And *I* want you to be safe."

At his words, Annie's troubled face cleared, and she smiled gratefully at Joe. "I guess that's why you're the Hardy I decided on," she teased, and gave him a happy kiss on the cheek.

It was around eleven when Joe and Annie climbed into the van and pulled away from the house.

"You hungry, Annie?" Joe asked.

She smiled ironically. "No, but I bet you are."

The first fast-food place they came to, they ordered and then ate as they drove along the highway. It's good being alone with Annie, Joe thought as he checked the rearview mirror and switched to the fast lane. Inside the van they were safe, in a warm and cozy cocoon far from the problems of the world.

With Annie so quiet Joe had time to do some serious thinking. He didn't like there being tension between Frank and him, but he knew that Annie was right when she said Frank had never liked her. And now Frank was doubly suspicious of her. It was also true that there were some facts about the case that just didn't add up. Maybe it was time to ask some questions.

"Annie, you asleep?" She turned to look at him and gently shook her head. "Can we talk?" This time she nodded. "That day in Mr. Pizza, when you got the phone call from Phil, that wasn't the first time you'd heard from him lately, was it?" Joe glanced over at her, curled up so sweetly in the seat beside him.

She hesitated but finally spoke. "No. Phil called me a few days earlier from New York. He wanted me to come to the city to see him. He said he'd hit the big time, and he wanted another chance with me."

"What did you tell him?"

"That I wanted nothing to do with him. Believe

me, Joe, I was through with Phil Sidler. I was afraid of him."

"But what happened? He wouldn't take no for an answer?"

"He said he was coming to talk to me. I begged him not to. I told him it wouldn't do any good, that I wouldn't see him." Annie twisted the ring on her right hand. "He wanted to know if there was anyone else."

"What did you tell him?"

"I knew he'd be jealous, Joe. If I mentioned another guy, he'd have a fit. So I lied. I told him no, but that I still didn't want to see him. He called again when he got to Bayport. He said he was coming to Mr. Pizza to get me. He said I'd change my mind when I heard about all the money he'd made."

"You think he was talking about the diamonds? That he'd double-crossed Cutter for the stones?"

"I don't know. I didn't ask where he'd gotten the money. He was always involved in some crazy get-rich scheme that only made him poorer, Joe." Annie reached out in the dark and put her hand on Joe's arm. "You believe me, don't you? I never knew how nice a guy could be until I met you. I'd never do anything to hurt you." In the beams from an oncoming car Annie's face was suddenly brightly lit, and Joe's heart did a flip-flop when he glanced at her gorgeous hazel eyes.

Annie snuggled closer to him. And Joe could

smell her cologne and shampoo as her hair softly brushed his cheek.

Joe hadn't thought he could ever care for anyone after Iola had been killed. But he had started feeling good about Annie. Now the accident had come between them. And he was beginning to have doubts about Annie's story. Some of it didn't add up.

His mind whirled with unanswered questions as he drove through the dark night. He glanced into the rearview mirror every few minutes to make sure they weren't being followed.

"Wake up, Annie." Joe gently roused the girl an hour later. "We're almost there."

"I wasn't asleep." Annie yawned. "I was thinking."

"About me?" Joe teased.

"I wish I'd met you years ago."

"Years ago I was just a kid," Joe had to admit.

"You're no old man now." Annie laughed. She looked out the window. "Why are we driving on these back streets?" She glanced into the sideview mirror, suddenly alert.

Joe had pulled off the highway at the exit for Allendale. He'd driven around the gray and deserted streets several times before heading for the motel he remembered. He didn't want to alarm Annie, but he was being realistic.

"I want to be sure no one's following us."

"You think they would? You think Cutter's

men could have been watching your house?" Annie's voice rose in alarm.

"Calm down, Annie. I said I was just being careful. No one's followed us. I've been watching all the way from Bayport."

"And I thought your mind was on me." Annie tried to smile, but Joe could see that she was still tense.

Pulling into the parking lot for the small motel, Joe managed a laugh. "Holiday Hideout." He read the name of the motel. "Like the sound of that?"

"It's hard to think of this as a holiday," Annie answered solemnly, looking at the neon vacancy sign.

They had to ring the bell to wake someone up so they could register. A woman unlocked the door. She was tying a bathrobe around her ample waist, her hair in rollers, her eyes heavy with sleep as she came out to greet them.

"Do you have a room left?" asked Joe.

The proprietor eyed the two of them, then smiled when she noticed Annie twisting her ring. Joe saw that she'd switched it to her left hand, and she was looking at him with dreamy eyes. He felt his face heat up. The woman laughed. "I can always spot honeymooners. I'll bet you two eloped, didn't you?" She reached under the desk and fumbled for the guest register. "I guess you'll only want the one night, won't you? Going on to Niagara Falls?''

Joe didn't know what to say. Honeymooners wouldn't choose to spend a week at the Holiday Hideout.

"We don't have much money, Mrs.—" Annie was asking for the woman's name.

"Booth. Edith Booth."

"Mrs. Booth. We can't go far. So we thought we'd find someplace clean and inexpensive and then take some day trips. I understand there are lakes near here where we can picnic."

"Why, sure. In the morning I'll give you a map and point out the places of interest. I understand starting out broke. Why, me and Earl, that's my husband, didn't have two quarters to rub together when we got married. But if you love each other—"

"Could I pay three nights in advance?" Joe interrupted the woman, who sounded as if she'd go on forever now that she'd decided to be friendly. "Then we'll see if we want to stay longer."

"That'd be fine." Edith Booth handed the pen to Joe.

He hesitated and glanced at Annie, who took his arm and smiled up at him. "Want me to write it, Joe?"

"No." Joe quickly scribbled Mr. and Mrs. Joe Hardy. This was getting ridiculous, he thought.

He paid cash and, after getting the key, hustled Annie out.

She burst into laughter the minute they got into the van to drive the short distance to the room. "Oh, Joe, you should have seen your face when I pretended we were married."

"Why did you do it, Annie?" he grumbled as he moved the van to Unit 10, the farthest from the office and the street, dark and shadowed except for the small light over the door. Mrs. Booth wanted them to have privacy.

"It was fun, Joe. But how will I explain it when she sees me alone tomorrow, though?"

"You can say we had our first fight and I left you because you're so conniving. Here's some money, Annie. I'll try to call every day." At least Annie's little game had made her forget about being afraid. Joe was glad for that.

He walked Annie to her room. "I hate to leave you here alone. Some husband, huh?" he teased.

"I'll be fine, Joe," Annie assured him. "My suitcase." She hurried back to the van. "I still think I should have left Bayport alone, though. I don't have much money, but if you'd have lent me some—what you're spending for the motel— I'd have paid you back when I got another job."

"I want you to be able to stay in Bayport, Annie." Joe pulled her close. "Frank and I will get to the bottom of this mess. Then you can go back to work and we'll take up where we left off—Mrs. Hardy.'' Joe laughed.

''Very touching,'' said a deep voice from the shadows. The tall man, the one Annie had so neatly disposed of, moved forward into the light. The single overhead bulb reflected off the gun that he had shoved into the small of Annie's back.

''You couldn't have followed us!'' Joe said, frustrated. He had taken every precaution. How had this man materialized out of the shadows just after they arrived?

''I'll take those diamonds, Annie. Back away and don't try anything,'' he said to Joe. ''Not if you want to see this girl alive in the morning.''

Chapter

11

"I DON'T HAVE any diamonds," Annie snapped.

"But you know where they are. I'll bet on it."
The tall man pushed on Annie's shoulder so she
was facing him now. There was no doubt that he
was in control. "My instincts are never wrong."

"Are you a friend of Phil's?" Annie asked.

Joe studied this man who was so persistent and
sure of himself. He didn't look like he'd be a
friend of Phil Sidler's. Tall, middle-aged, graying
slightly at the temples, he might have been a
college professor or a businessman.

Maybe he had found out about the robbery and
decided this was an easy way to make his fortune.
Or maybe he headed a rival gang and the two
were fighting over this haul. That was it, Joe
decided. The guy had to be a rival of Cutter's.

Joe was trying to identify his slight accent, although he wasn't sure what good that would do.

"Who are you?" Joe insisted.

"A concerned party." The man pointed toward the van with the gun. When Annie didn't move right away, he gave her a quick shove with the flat of his hand.

Joe had no choice but to climb back into the van with Annie. The tall man settled himself in the seat behind Joe and Annie so he could keep the gun trained on her.

"Back to Bayport, Joe," he instructed. "I'll leave my rental car here."

So he'd been watching the house and he'd followed them the whole way. Joe felt like an incompetent beginner. How had the guy done it? And how did he know where they lived? They had left him unconscious in that parking garage in New York City.

Joe glanced at his gas gauge. It was approaching empty. Good. What would this man be able to do with a car out of gas on the highway in the middle of the night?

"What good will it do us to return to Bayport?" Joe asked, trying to get the guy to talk. Maybe he'd let something slip.

"We're going on a little treasure hunt with Annie planning the itinerary. Someone has three million dollars' worth of diamonds, and I want them."

"Three million?" Joe whistled. No wonder the thieves were so insistent.

"Three million?" Annie echoed.

"It doesn't take that many diamonds if they're quality ones. They could be hidden in a very small space." Joe decided that the tall man knew what he was talking about.

"You think Phil Sidler had them? That he really did double-cross Cutter and his men?" Joe asked.

The man relaxed back into his seat. He seemed willing to talk, but Joe noticed that he kept the gun leveled at Annie. "Phil did have them at first," he said. "But they weren't in his hotel at Bayport or in his apartment in New York. We're still looking for them. Logic tells me that Phil either gave them to Annie or that he told her where they were hidden."

"How many times do I have to tell people I have no idea what's going on here?" Annie protested. "Phil told me nothing, and I certainly don't have three million dollars' worth of diamonds or I wouldn't be here."

"If Phil had told Annie anything, she'd have told the police," said Joe. "Wouldn't you, Annie?"

"Of course I would." Annie turned her head and stared out her window.

Joe was not so sure. Three million dollars would tempt almost anyone, he thought. He was at a point where he didn't know what to believe, so he concentrated on driving. Until he thought of a plan, he wasn't in control of the situation anyway.

"Of course, it is possible that the hiding place of the jewels died with Phil," the man in the backseat said.

"Who *are* you?" Joe asked again. "You're not in Cutter's gang. You're not a friend of Phil's. What's your connection with all this? Are you part of a tour group? Did you miss your bus?"

The man smiled. He seemed pleased by Joe's defiance. "Let's just say that I'm trying to return the diamonds to their rightful owner."

"And who is that?" Joe turned slightly, only to see the gun raised and aimed at him.

This time there was no answer. They drove a few miles in silence and then, "Slow down, Joe. Drive the minimum speed for a few miles."

Joe sighed, resigning himself to following orders until he was in a position to disarm their passenger. He slowed the van to forty miles an hour, a mere crawl on the turnpike. There was no traffic on the highway now. The clock in the van read two A.M.

"Can I turn on the radio?" Joe asked with some sarcasm in his voice.

"Forget it," the man barked.

Glancing in the rearview mirror, Joe noticed a single pair of lights behind the van. He wondered why the car wasn't passing. No one drove forty on the turnpike—not even little old ladies.

"Speed up," came the voice from behind him. "Drive about five miles over the speed limit but no more. We don't need the highway patrol pulling us over."

Joe pressed his foot down on the accelerator and sped up. As he guessed it would, the car behind them kept pace.

"Just as I thought," the tall man said, looking worried. "Trouble."

Annie looked in the sideview mirror. All she could see were a pair of headlights. "It's Cutter," she said. "Hurry, Joe. Don't let him get me again. He threatened me before. If he catches me again, he'll kill me, Joe. I know he will.

"Annie." She was practically hysterical. "Stay calm, Annie. I won't let them get you."

In compliance with the tall man's orders, he continued slowing down and speeding up, sometimes placing his foot on the brake abruptly. As the cat-and-mouse game continued, Joe tried to relieve his impatience by reviewing the situation.

He'd made a mistake bringing Annie upstate. Both of them could have been safe in the Hardys' home right then. Now it looked as if Joe might be responsible for her death—and possibly his own. If Cutter's men were following, they'd be playing hardball this time. There'd be no easy escape.

Had their escape earlier been a farce, anyway?

Had Cutter let them go, planning to tail them until Annie led him to the diamonds? Joe realized with a sudden shock that he now believed she had the jewels. He must be tired. The only thing he knew for sure was that they wouldn't stop at anything to regain that fortune.

The next time Joe slowed down, the car behind them pulled up beside the van. The driver tried to force Joe off the road. But Joe swung left onto the shoulder, then swerved hard to the right and speeded up, leaving the other car behind.

"Any suggestions?" Joe asked, sarcasm in his voice. "You're in charge of this little game."

"I hadn't planned on Cutter's following us," the man answered.

Joe was tensed for action as he sped off into the tunnel of light that his headlights cut into the dark. He pulled into the passing lane and drove faster.

"One of them has a gun, Joe!" Annie screamed. The car had pulled up beside them on her side. "An Uzi. He's going to shoot."

Joe didn't think the guy would shoot Annie if he believed she knew where the diamonds were. But better not take chances. Flicking a switch, he brought bulletproof panels down to cover all of the windows. Now Joe could use the van almost as a tank. He slowed, then glanced into the other lane. Speeding up, he left the smaller car far behind.

Now the only thing he had to worry about was their shooting out his tires.

Annie said, glancing at Joe, "I'm starting to believe maybe you *can* take care of us."

Deftly weaving from lane to lane so the guys behind him couldn't get a clear shot at his tires, Joe became aware of every muscle in his body. He hungered for action, a real confrontation to end this chase. But instead he called up his powers of patience.

He knew that eventually the state police would have to pull him over. The way he was driving he *had* to attract attention—at least that was what he was hoping. And when the police did stop him, the car behind them wouldn't stick around. But with the kind of luck Joe was having lately, the trooper on duty would be taking a coffee break. Not much action in the wee hours of the morning.

Joe pressed his speed higher and higher, continuing to weave back and forth. He guessed the guys pursuing them weren't going to shoot because they would have gotten off a couple of rounds already. They didn't want to risk Annie in an accident.

"Good idea, Joe," the voice behind him commented. "Attracting the state police is smart. In fact, the police do seem to be the perfect answer here. Take the next exit."

The man had to be bluffing. He couldn't really want the law to stop them. But Joe decided that the tall man must have figured that if their action got Cutter's men off their tail, he was all for it.

"Hang on," he said to Annie. He needn't have bothered. She was clutching the door in a death grip.

Joe braked and took the off ramp at a speed that sent the van careening dangerously. Without stopping, he made a right-hand turn that led eventually onto the main street of a small town. The small car fell behind.

The streets of the town were brightly lit but devoid of people. One all-night gas station was closed up tight. But they were in luck. A policeman sat in his patrol car in the parking lot of a local café. Probably he had been dozing or listening to his radio, but he came to life when Joe shot by.

Light swirling, siren screaming, he pulled out after the van. Gratefully Joe pulled up to the curb, flipping a switch to roll the window shields down. He'd take the ticket gladly. He was happy, though, that Frank had been driving in New York City. Both the Hardys' driving records were getting badly tarnished by this case.

"Tell him you want to go to the station. Say you have an incident to report. And don't try getting away—either of you," their passenger growled.

Before Joe could react to the stranger's surprising behavior, the policeman was at his window.

"Out for a little drive, are you?" he asked as Joe rolled his window down and handed him his license.

"Sir, I can explain. There was an incident on the highway that I need to report. A car tried to run us off the road. My friend here and I felt we were in danger."

"Please help us," Annie added in a voice that was still filled with fear.

The officer looked at Joe's license, then handed it back slowly. "All right. But this had better be good. Third street, turn left, second building on the right, back entrance. I'll be right behind you, so don't try any funny stuff."

"No, sir," said Joe, and groaned with relief after the officer turned away. He'd tried all the funny stuff he knew earlier.

"Very good, Joe. You sounded very much like a law-abiding citizen. And our friends have stopped following us."

Right, Joe thought, and the first person to be reported to the police will be you. If he played his cards right, they'd be rid of both opponents in a couple of minutes. But Joe wondered why the tall man was being so cooperative. Why was he going along to the station? Didn't he know Joe would turn him in?

The station was empty except for one dispatcher and one clerk, a woman in uniform at the front desk. Joe and Annie headed for the desk, followed by the police officer and the tall man.

The tall man had pocketed his gun as they got out of the car and seemed to have forgotten that he and Annie were there. After Joe arrived at the front desk with Annie, he noticed that their kidnapper had stopped the officer to talk with him in private. After a brief conversation, the two headed down the corridor and into a room; the door quickly closed behind them.

"Miss," Joe said to the officer at the desk. "That man in there with the patrolman, he's armed and has been holding us captive."

She looked at Joe as if he were hallucinating but picked up the phone and punched in an extension.

"I see. Thank you," she said after reporting Joe's accusation and listening a moment. "You're to wait here," she instructed Joe and Annie. "Sit down anywhere. It'll be a few minutes."

Joe felt as if he were being left out, and he felt he had every right to know what was happening. Also he discovered he was exhausted. He'd give anything to wake up and discover he'd been dreaming the whole incident. He followed Annie to a group of chairs, but instead of sitting down, he headed past them toward the closed door where the officer and the tall man had disappeared.

"Sir, I'll have to ask you to be seated." The policewoman's sharp voice stopped Joe.

"But—"

"Those are my orders. I suggest you comply."

Joe sat and crossed his legs at the ankles. Nervously he tapped one foot up and down in a frantic rhythm. Annie sat flipping through the pages of a magazine, as though she were casually waiting for an appointment. Only a slight tremor in her hand revealed her anxiety and fatigue.

"What do you think's going on, Joe?" she whispered to him finally.

"I have no idea. And I don't like not knowing. We've been here over half an hour."

Finally Joe returned to the desk to demand some information. "Officer." He had to speak to get her attention. She acted as if he were invisible.

"Yes?" She walked over to the counter where Joe was standing and fuming.

"I'd like to see the man who came in here with us."

"What man?" the woman asked as if she'd never seen Joe before.

"When the officer brought us in, there was a very tall man with us. He was over six-six. I'd like to see him, Officer Lloyd," Joe said, reading the woman's name tag.

"I'm sorry, there's no one here of that description."

"But—I came in with him." No tall man? Joe couldn't believe it. "At least let me talk to the officer who brought us in."

"He's not here, either. He went out to answer a call."

"He's gone?" What was going on? "Look, Officer. I was brought in here for a traffic violation. You can't keep me all night. Just give me my ticket and I'll leave."

"Oh, I'm sorry, sir. Didn't anyone tell you? You're free to go. I have no information about a violation. It must have been dropped."

Joe was too stunned to move for several seconds. Finally he did spin around and stride back to Annie.

"Come on, we're getting out of here."

"What's going on? Where's the tall man?"

"I have no idea, but I'm not going to argue with anyone because I'm not getting a ticket. This is bizarre."

Annie didn't question the reason for their freedom. "I'm exhausted, Joe. Can we go back to your place? I felt safe there."

"My plan exactly. So far we've gotten nowhere—fast. And I have an appointment at ten in the morning—this morning."

Outside the station the sky was beginning to lighten. Before they got in the van, Joe checked it over carefully but found no evidence of tampering. Also there was no sign of the man who'd held them captive on the wild ride down the highway. It was as if he had never existed, and the incident had never happened.

He glanced around the small, quiet town, but it seemed empty. No one had started leaving for work yet; no joggers were pounding the streets. There was no sign of the car that had followed them.

"Who was that man?" Annie asked out loud. "And where did he go? I don't understand why he keeps appearing and disappearing."

"I'd like to know what story he told the police," Joe said. "But right now, I'm starving. It's almost light. We can at least have breakfast before we go."

Joe pulled the van in front of the café that now was open. The aromas of freshly brewed coffee and bacon frying greeted them when they entered. "I'll take a number one and a number four," Joe told the waitress at the counter, and handed the menu to Annie. "To go."

"Are you sure that'll be enough, Joe?" Annie smiled. "I'm not sharing. I'm starving, too." She gave the waitress her order.

They each drank a cup of coffee while they waited, and Joe ate two sweet rolls. Then he handed the bag to Annie and paid for the food. A couple of sleepy men wandered in as they walked out. Joe glanced in all directions, then climbed into the van. He felt almost relaxed as he swung onto the highway. Now was the time to ask Annie some serious questions.

"I must say, Joe Hardy," Annie started before he had a chance, "spending the night with you is not boring."

Joe didn't laugh, and Annie looked over to see why.

"Sorry, Annie. I've got some bad news—the excitement may not be over." Joe's two big breakfasts turned to lead in his stomach. "We may have lost the mysterious stranger, but I don't think we've lost Cutter."

Annie stared into the sideview mirror, her face slowly turning into a mask of pure terror. "No, Joe! We can't let them get us. I know them! They'll force me to talk and then they'll kill me!"

Chapter

12

JOE SPED UP in a desperate attempt to get away, but the car behind them was determined not to lose its quarry again. Pulling alongside Joe, the chase car kept pace with Joe.

"Joe, they're pointing Uzis at us!" Annie screamed, and ducked down in her seat.

Joe again flicked the switch that brought down the bulletproof shields. The round of bullets hitting the van spurred him on. The bullets were obviously being aimed at the van's tires now. The men must have decided to chance killing Annie for the opportunity to talk to her. Surviving this assault, Joe decided, would be a matter of blind luck.

"We're dead, Joe." Annie was crumpled up in the seat beside Joe.

"Hang on, Annie. I can lose them—I promise. I know the area. My dad used to bring us fishing around here."

Joe swung off the expressway. The car chasing them sped by, brakes squealing. Almost immediately after the exit ramp, Joe took a narrow dirt road that led to a thickly forested plot of land. The road, a one-lane rutted path, wound upward, and the van bounced and skidded until Joe was forced to slow down.

The road became narrower and steeper until it leveled out and headed downhill. It was on the downhill side that the van began to cough.

"What the—" Joe glared at all the gauges. What he saw made his heart sink. "Oh, no!"

"What's wrong?" Annie asked.

"We're out of gas." Joe grinned sheepishly.

"Out of gas? Joe, you're kidding. How could you run out of gas?"

"Easy. I had a lot on my mind." He looked around quickly, his mind clicking now. As the van coasted to a stop, he maneuvered it off the road. "Come on, we're bailing out."

"Joe, there's no place to go."

"Sure there is." He turned off the ignition. Deep forest surrounded them. After jumping out, Joe locked the van. He had no choice but to leave it. Cutter's car had no doubt made a U-turn by now and was headed in their direction. The van wasn't hidden completely, but someone would have to know where to look to see it.

Joe reached for Annie's hand, and within seconds they were in the forest, hidden by trees and brush. The birds immediately grew silent, aware of the intrusion. But a squirrel overhead scolded, complaining about the visitors.

The ground crunched with each step because of the carpet of leaves underfoot. To Joe they sounded like a couple of bears crashing about, and there was no way to be quiet. Any minute Cutter's thugs could catch up and hone in on them.

Annie wobbled along beside him. It was all she could do to keep upright. Joe looked at her shoes. She still had on the high heels.

"Take them off," he advised.

"It would be even slower going. I can't run barefoot."

"Why don't girls wear sensible shoes?"

"I didn't know we were going for a hike in the woods," Annie complained.

Joe clutched Annie's hand tightly and slowed down. He was looking for a clearing not too far from where they'd left the van. Just past the clearing there was a small fishing cabin he and his father had rented some years earlier. If they could find the cabin, if it was still there, they could take refuge, or at least stop and assess their situation.

"I'm sorry, Joe." Annie's breath came in short bursts. "I can't go much farther without resting. If they followed us—"

"They would have caught up by now, Annie." Joe tried to reassure her. He felt sure they were being followed, but he didn't know how far behind Cutter's men were, or how good they were at tracking. There were several ways he and Annie could have headed from the van. With any luck, the men could have taken a wrong trail or split up, leaving the odds better for Joe.

Joe swore at himself under his breath. He was a fool, stupid and careless—an amateur. How could he run out of gas. They'd had a head start when the chase car had flown past the exit. Maybe he and Annie could have gotten across the dirt road to the state highway, then pulled into one of the little towns over there and hidden out. Any number of small roads crisscrossed these wooded hills, and Joe knew most of them. Sometimes, bored with fishing, he and Frank had ridden dirt bikes for miles.

But he couldn't dwell on what might have been. He needed a plan for escaping Cutter's men now. And if he could successfully overpower them, how could he and Annie get back to town? Cutter's car. That was it. Ambush them and take their car.

"Annie." Joe pulled her into a small clearing and behind an outcropping of rocks. "I've got a plan. We're going to stop and wait for them. You stay here. I'm going to see if I can find another place to hide."

"Joe, don't leave me alone," Annie pleaded.

"I'm not leaving. Get back behind those rocks and keep your eyes open. And keep that karate chop ready."

Hunched down, Joe ran for a thick tree. He paused, listened, heard nothing. Maybe they weren't being followed. A short distance away a small stream bubbled and slid over rocks. A thrush sang in sweet, melodious tones. Joe was pleased to hear it, since its presence meant no one was disturbing the bird.

Circling back the way they'd come, careful to plant his feet on grass or rocks rather than dry leaves, he listened. Nothing.

He was on the verge of deciding that he and Annie were alone when a scream pierced the air. At the same time a shot rang out.

"Annie!" he yelled, and dashed back to where he'd left her.

She had been struggling with a man, and was just throwing him to the ground when Joe reached her.

The man rolled over, jumped up, and whirled at Joe's approach. Annie was reaching for a rock to hit him on the head when three men crashed out of the woods behind her and shouted, "Hold it—right there."

One man had an Uzi pointed straight at Annie. Another trained his weapon on Joe. The third lowered his gun and picked up the .44 Magnum his partner had dropped when he'd fallen to the ground.

"What's the matter, Clive?" the thug with the machine gun said. "Can't handle a little girl?"

"This is no ordinary girl, pal. Take my word for it. You tie her up." He grabbed Annie's arms. She struggled, her eyes pleading with Joe to help her.

Before Joe could move, two of the other men slammed him to the ground. Twisting loose, Joe rolled and kicked upward, catching one man in the stomach. Even so, his two attackers finally managed to pin him facedown. Then Joe felt a small circle of cold steel against his neck.

"We have orders not to kill you, kid, but we might just forget. So lie still."

"You could say it was an accident," the man called Hodge gasped. He'd helped wrestle Joe to the ground and was nursing a bruised solar plexus. "Your gun went off in a struggle."

"Please, don't kill him!" Annie demanded. "You've got me. Let him go."

"Let him go, lady? You've got to be kidding."

Joe's fear for Annie forced him to make one more try for freedom. If he could get the machine gun . . . Twisting out from under the man who held him captive, Joe kept low, then hacked at his wrist with a powerful blow. The gun flew from the man's hand, but just as Joe closed his hand around the weapon, the butt of a gun slammed into his head from behind. Through a burst of stars, Joe heard Annie scream. Then he toppled onto the forest floor.

It was hours later when sunlight streamed into the clearing, warming Joe's stiff body. His temples pulsed in a wave of pain. His head felt as if it were filled with lead pellets. He managed to focus his eyes, but he could move neither his arms nor legs. Both were tied securely behind him. Slowly, Joe forced himself to raise his head as the world around him flashed and wavered like a gruesome light show. Pain and fear struck his gut like a lightning bolt.

The fear was not for himself. It was for Annie. Cutter's thugs were gone, and they had taken the girl with them.

Joe had failed to protect her—and for Annie his failure meant certain death.

Chapter

13

A BLUE JAY shrilled overhead as if laughing at Joe's predicament. Two squirrels chattered, chasing each other down the bark of a nearby tree. Each sound made his headache worse.

Yet Joe couldn't lie there suffering. That wasn't doing him or Annie any good. He used the pain like a whip to bring himself to a state of alertness and to remain conscious.

Slowly Joe rocked from side to side, trying to gain the momentum he needed to turn over. The movement only twisted the ropes tighter, making them cut into his wrists and ankles. Finally, he flipped over onto his back, biting his lip to keep from crying out as the ropes cut deeper into his already raw skin.

He managed to sit up and look around. He saw

nothing that he might use to cut through the cords. He was no longer near the rocks where Annie had hidden, but near the creek now.

If his memory served him correctly, there were rocks clustered all up and down the stream bed. He used to climb on the rocks years ago.

Fatigue threatened to eliminate the surge of adrenaline he'd mustered by turning over. Annie's in trouble, he reminded himself. And it's my fault. How long had he been unconscious? Not too long, he thought, since the sun was still low in the east. There was a chance to find her if he could get out of there soon.

He debated whether or not it would be faster to roll or scoot down to the stream. Scooting won since it was the less painful of the two. But twice he lost his balance and rolled when he would have preferred to move in the slower manner.

Finally he reached his goal. There were plenty of sharp edges in the jumble of rock piles beside the stream, left there by some long-ago shift in the mountainous terrain.

Joe's mouth was so parched he could scarcely swallow, and the water teased him. It was so near, yet he couldn't reach it. He had to get loose first. Again he endured the agony as he lifted his hands behind his back to the edge of a rock and began to slide the rope back and forth.

It took less time than he'd anticipated once he

got a rhythm going. The granite was razor sharp where a piece had broken away long ago.

When he felt his bonds release, he gave a sigh of relief. Quickly he brought his arms, stiff and sore, around to his ankles to untie the cord there. He rolled to the creek, drank deeply, then ducked his head into the cold water to clear his cobwebby brain.

His muscles screamed as he stood, but he insisted that his legs move until he reached the road.

The van was still hidden beside the small dirt road, but it was useless to Joe. There were flares in a toolbox in the back, but no one was likely to be driving by so early in the day. Joe checked his watch, but it was crushed and broken. Apparently, he had smashed it during the fight with Cutter's men. Joe took off on foot for the highway.

He was sweating profusely from the pace he'd maintained when he came in sight of the highway. Never had morning rush-hour traffic looked so good. One, it suggested that it was not so late as Joe had feared. Two, with all these people out there, someone had to pick him up.

Or would they? He must look awful. That was it. He'd play on looking awful. Taking a handkerchief from his pocket, miraculously still white, he dabbed it in the fresh blood on his wrists that were rubbed raw enough to bleed. Then he tied it around his head. Stepping back off the road, he searched until he found a dead limb of sufficient length and strength to fashion into a crutch.

He climbed the embankment to the expressway and went into his act. Placing the crook of the limb under his armpit, he limped in an exaggerated manner, using the limb to partially support himself. Then he turned and stuck out his thumb.

No one stopped. While he didn't blame them— he rarely picked up hitchhikers—he thought surely they could see that he had been injured.

Suppressing the desire to either run out into the road and wave someone down or scream at the cars whizzing by, he continued to wave and thumb for a ride.

Finally a station wagon did pull over just ahead of him.

"Have a problem, young man?" To Joe's surprise, his rescuer was an elderly woman. She sat ramrod straight in the driver's seat, her white hair piled high on her head.

"Yes, ma'am. I wrecked my car back on that dirt road." He motioned toward the woods. "Hit a rock in the road as I came over a hill. I need to get some help."

"Get in, young man. You must have been driving awfully fast to have gotten hurt that badly. I'll bet you weren't wearing your seat belt, were you? You young people think nothing bad can ever happen to you."

116

Lady, Joe said to himself, you'd never believe how many bad things I've seen.

He grinned sheepishly at her. "Well, I guess I was being a little careless. I was thinking about the good fishing back there in those streams. I really appreciate your stopping. I was afraid no one was going to pull over."

"Normally I wouldn't. I never pick up hitchhikers. Most of them are jailbirds. But you look like my brother Homer's grandson, Peter Hobbs. You don't know Peter, do you?"

"No, ma'am." They continued driving and talking for another hour. Joe couldn't believe he was sitting there making small talk with this woman. But at least she was driving the speed limit, and by some rare bit of luck she was headed to Bayport also.

"Decided to go live in the city, he did," she said, picking up the thread of conversation she had dropped an hour earlier. "Said he could get a job in New York. Don't know why anyone'd want to live in the city, though. Peter took a job as a policeman," the old woman continued. "Don't know why anyone would want to be a policeman."

Police! Joe groaned. His appointment with the Bayport police.

"Are you hurting?" the woman asked when she heard Joe's groan. "Should I take you to a hospital?"

"No, ma'am. I'll be all right. I just remembered something. What time is it?"

"Near nine o'clock. I've got plenty of time. My dentist appointment's at ten right here in Bayport, and then I thought I'd do some shopping at the Bayport mall. Maybe take in a movie. Not too many movies I like to see these days, but I do like a good cry or a love story."

"I don't suppose you'd have time to drop me at High Street and Elm, would you, ma'am?" Joe interrupted gently.

"Why, that's very near my dentist. Maybe your luck is changing." The woman laughed softly, and a pleased look came onto her face.

Joe certainly needed a change in luck. "Yes, ma'am, I hope so. I'm lucky you weren't afraid to pick me up."

"That's right," she agreed, and slowed up to pull up against the curb. "This close enough to where you need to go?"

"Sure is, ma'am." Joe unlatched the car door. "And thanks again."

"You're welcome. Maybe you should see a doctor."

"I will." Joe slammed the door and waved. He limped until she drove out of sight, then tossed his crutch into a nearby trash basket and sprinted home.

With any more of the luck his rescuer mentioned he could get home, shower, call a cab, and get to the police station in plenty of time. What he had to decide before he got there was how much of this story to tell Officer O'Hara. Would she believe any of it? Could the police find Annie any sooner than he could?

Nearing the Hardy home, Joe pulled up short. His luck must have run out. Stopping on a lawn two doors from his house, he stared.

A police car was parking in front of his place. It looked like Officer O'Hara in the driver's seat. What had happened to bring her here instead of waiting for Joe at the station? And what would she do when she found Joe gone?

Chapter

14

FRANK HARDY STOOD in the doorway of his house trying to make a decision. He knew Joe wasn't home, and he didn't know how long he could cover for him.

"Good morning, Officer O'Hara. Officer Riley," he said, trying to be pleasant. It was good Con was there; maybe he could defuse any unpleasantness. "What brings you here so early?"

"This is not a social call, Mr. Hardy." Officer O'Hara was all business. "I suspect you know that. I'm here to see your brother."

"He had a bad night." Frank stalled, wondering where Joe could be. He knew that his taking off with Annie was a bad idea. But his appointment with the police wasn't until ten. "I knew his appointment wasn't until ten so I didn't wake him. Is something wrong?"

"That's what I'm here to find out. We got a call at the station telling us Joe had left town. Was he skipping out on his bail?"

"Who told you that?" Frank asked.

"The call was anonymous. But I decided it was worth following up." Officer O'Hara was growing impatient.

"Joe is innocent, Officer O'Hara, and he's cooperated with you from the beginning. Why would he have any reason to skip out?"

"That's what I want to find out."

Frank took the risk of being blunt even though he didn't want to annoy Officer O'Hara any further. She already believed that Joe was a murderer.

"Excuse me for saying so, Officer, but I think your time could be better spent finding the people who are really responsible for Phil Sidler's death. The jewel thieves. It's obvious there's a connection there."

"Are you telling me how to do my job now?" O'Hara started past Frank into the foyer.

Officer Con Riley followed her in with an apologetic shrug and a rueful smile for Frank. Frank read the gestures to say he'd better produce Joe and satisfy the young officer's curiosity.

"Do you have a search warrant, Officer

O'Hara?'' Frank asked, politely but firmly blocking her entry into the living room.

"Do I need one, Mr. Hardy?'' O'Hara asked back.

Frank finally gave in and sighed. He'd protected Joe as long as he could. "Joe's room is upstairs.'' He followed O'Hara, however, prepared to keep talking.

Officer O'Hara marched briskly up the stairway and down the hall. She knocked sharply on the door Frank indicated and smiled grimly when she got no answer. Twisting the knob, she strode in. Frank was shocked to see Joe's bed a jumble of blankets and the spread in a pile on the floor.

He didn't even try to hide a relieved grin as the bathroom door opened.

"Officer O'Hara,'' Joe Hardy said, his face a picture of surprised innocence. "I thought my appointment was at ten. Get anxious to see me?'' Joe's timing was perfect, his entrance suspiciously well planned. He strolled in from his bathroom, wrapped only in a long towel, hair wet and tousled. He was perfectly decent, but he wasn't dressed for greeting guests. He held another towel to hide his scraped wrists.

Officer O'Hara stepped back, completely flustered. "Oh—I—'' she stammered. Then she regained her composure. ":Excuse me, Mr. Hardy, there was no answer to my knock on your door, and I had been led to believe—''

"Believe what, Officer?" Joe grinned, pretending to be unaware of the woman's embarrassment. "That I'd forgotten my appointment with you? I was just getting ready."

"Fine, Mr. Hardy. I'll wait while you finish dressing and give you a ride." Officer O'Hara spun around quickly and left the room, followed by a greatly amused Con Riley. He didn't say anything to Joe or Frank, but he didn't have to.

"Joe, where have you been?" asked Frank when he was alone with his brother. He had enjoyed Joe's act so much that he had trouble sounding angry.

"Frank, listen, I'm going to talk fast." Joe turned immediately serious. "The van is on that little dirt road we used to take when we went fishing with Dad. North of here about an hour."

For the first time Frank noticed the abrasions on Joe's wrists. He stepped forward, taking Joe's hand. "What happened? You need to see a doctor."

"There isn't time. I'll pour some antiseptic over them when I'm dressed. Our elusive tall man forced Annie and me to return to Bayport, but Cutter's men caught up to us before we could get here. They've taken Annie, Frank. We've got to help her."

"I had to swear to Dad I wouldn't go back to Cutter's hideout. Not without New York City cops. He's going to contact some of his old buddies on the force today and set everything in motion.''

''Then I'll have to go alone, Frank. Annie's life is in danger now—not later.''

''Tell the Bayport police the whole story, Joe,'' Frank urged.

''Getting Annie out of there is my number-one priority, Frank, but you know as well as I do that we've got to find the diamonds—to connect Phil to the robberies. And to clear Annie and then me. I want you go get the van. Take a can of gas.''

''You ran out of *gas?*'' asked Frank.

''I don't want to hear it, Frank. Just go get the van.'' Joe rummaged through a drawer.

''I have a better idea.'' Frank paced the floor while Joe dressed. ''I'll send a tow truck for the van, and we'll borrow Callie's car. It'd take too much time to go out and get the van right now.''

''I will report Annie missing, and I won't interfere with the NYPD, but I think it's up to us to find her. Dad would understand that.''

Back in the bathroom Joe poured some hydrogen peroxide over his wrists, wincing as the antiseptic bubbled and fizzed in the scrapes and cuts. He shrugged off the bandages that Frank pulled from the medicine cabinet. ''Don't need them. Pick me up at the station in half an hour.'' Joe ran down the stairs.

Frank used Joe's extension phone to make his calls.

"Of course you can borrow my car, Frank," said Callie when he reached her. "But I'm going along. I'm tired of never seeing you."

"This may be dangerous, Callie. I don't want you along."

"I don't care what you want, Frank. I can drive. You may need me. I won't go inside, but I'll keep the engine running."

Frank knew better than to argue with Callie when she was in that mood. Besides, she might be right. They could need her if they had to make a quick getaway. Cutter's men and the tall man, whoever he was, knew the van. They wouldn't be looking for Callie's car.

Callie picked Frank up and they drove to the police station. Joe was already pacing the sidewalk outside.

"Rehash of the whole case," he explained as he hopped in the back seat of Callie's little green car. "That's all they wanted to do. Waste of time. They didn't even want to hear what happened yesterday. I told them I hadn't been able to locate Annie, but they weren't concerned."

"I guess even they're convinced she's part of the gang," Frank said. "But they can't do anything until they get some hard evidence against her."

While Frank wanted Annie safe, he did remind Joe that Annie, if involved, had gotten herself into this mess.

"Ready for a little trip to New York City, Callie?" asked Frank as they hopped into the car.

"Filled the tank before I picked you up. You navigate." She spun efficiently out of the lot and headed for the expressway.

"I'm glad you remembered to get gas," said Frank, looking at Joe and hoping to get a smile. But Joe stared into the distance as though he hadn't heard what Frank said.

Frank and Joe reviewed all they knew about the case on the way to the city, but what they arrived at was that they had no concrete evidence that would convict Cutter. And that the identity of the tall man was still a mystery. His involvement in the case seemed to be independent of the police or the jewel thieves.

"Find a space or double-park, Callie," Frank instructed as they entered the underground lot that held the key to Cutter's hideout. "Head the car for the exit and wait. We might need to get out of here fast."

"If we ever get inside." Joe seemed less optimistic than Frank about finding the secret for getting upstairs to Cutter's secret apartment.

Facing the solid concrete wall, Frank and Joe didn't know where to start looking. Somewhere there was a hidden panel, a button, or switch, that brought down and opened an elevator large enough for a car. The limo seemed to have disappeared into thin air, so that had to be the explanation.

The wall was cold to the touch and rough-textured. Frank patted, punched, searched, having started at the middle and headed right. Joe, beside him, moved to the left, fingering the solid wall in the same manner.

In a matter of minutes, they met back in the center where they'd started. "Nothing," both agreed.

"There has to be someplace we haven't touched, some combination," Joe said. He pounded the wall with his fist in frustration.

"That's a fairly astute assumption, boys," a voice behind them said.

"What—you—" Joe and Frank swung around as one. They had been too intent on the wall to realize they were being watched.

"What a nice surprise to find you here, Joe." The tall man, looking weary and dressed in very rumpled clothing, leaned casually on a green Chevy—one of the only cars in the garage.

His smile was casual, almost gentle.

But the 9mm Beretta in his hand was all business.

Chapter

15

"YOU BOYS ARE in good company," the tall man continued. "I couldn't find the combination to get inside, either. My real hope was that one of Cutter's men would come down and show it to me."

"What do you mean? You left us there in that police station," said Joe. "What did you tell them, anyway?"

"I asked them to stall you for as long as possible, thinking that if Cutter's men thought you'd reported them to the police, they'd give up on you—for then. I showed my credentials to the officer and explained the situation. It didn't work, though. By the time I got a ride from one of the officers back to my car and returned, I saw Cutter's thugs follow you out of town."

"If you're so all-seeing, Mr. Wise Guy, I guess you saw them tie me up and leave with Annie."

"I didn't know you weren't in their car. I just saw the car pull off the road and then return. I assumed you were in the car with Annie. I followed them back to the city, but unfortunately I lost them in traffic on the way back. By the time I got here, they'd done their disappearing act."

Joe started to lunge for the man, but Frank stopped him. "Settle down, Joe. We don't have time to fight with someone who might be on the same side we are. Why don't you put your gun away, whoever you are. Admit it—you haven't gotten any further than we have. At least we've been inside this place."

"True. And you did leave in one piece. Luck, maybe."

"Who *are* you?" Joe was willing to talk only if he knew who he was talking to. "You showed the police something convincing. Why don't you try your credentials out on us?"

The tall man slipped his gun into a shoulder holster inside his suit jacket. Then he held out his hand. "Brookshier. Selden Brookshier. CSO."

Frank shook hands, but Joe ignored the man's friendly gesture. "CSO?" Frank asked.

"Central Selling Organization—out of London. Diamonds. That last shipment was ours, and we frown on people killing our couriers and helping themselves to our property. This sight never arrived."

"Sight?" Frank questioned. "I thought we were looking for diamonds."

"A sight is a package of rough diamonds purchased by one of our clients, usually a dealer or a diamond cutter," Selden Brookshier explained. "The value of a parcel averages about a million dollars. This one happened to be worth three times that."

"Do the Bayport police know you're here?" Frank asked. "Are you working with them?" That must have been how Brookshier walked into Phil's room. He'd stopped at the police station and picked up a key.

"Yes, but as you've seen, I try to keep a very low profile. The fewer people who know who I am, the better. We don't like any publicity about our shipments. The more people who know about them, the more likely we are to become targets for thieves. We suspect someone on the inside told Phil Sidler—who at the time worked for Cutter—of this delivery. A woman who worked for the dealer."

"Annie?" Frank said.

"Exactly. She handled the correspondence and plane tickets. She knew her employer had viewed the stones, sent the check for them to London, and was expecting them. She wouldn't know the exact delivery time, since we don't say, but all that took on her part was a little patience.''

"You're guessing." Joe didn't want to hear that Annie was involved in the robbery. "Do you have any evidence that Annie was involved?"

"No more evidence than we have against Cutter, but it all adds up. We attribute half or more of the jewelry jobs in this state to Cutter and his gang. We've caught people who work for him, but never Cutter or any of the higher-ups. We've never gotten enough evidence on Cutter that we thought would stick. Annie and Phil may have done us a favor in the long run, but neither may live to be thanked. I doubt if anyone lives to brag about double-crossing Cutter.''

"We've got to get Annie out," said Joe, suddenly realizing that time might be running out for his friend.

"Come on." Frank returned to searching the rough concrete wall, starting to feel a sense of frustration knowing that they were near Cutter's hideout.

"Of course!" Frank said suddenly. "We should have been using our eyes instead of our sense of touch. Look here." He pointed to what might be mistaken as a grease spot on the gray wall.

Pressing on the spot started the sound of whirring, grinding, and purring. Slowly, large double doors, wide enough for a car to drive through, opened before them. The trio hopped inside and looked over the selection panel. "Any suggestions?" asked Frank.

"Start with One," Joe suggested. "We don't have to get off if it's wrong."

The elevator was painfully slow. Frank hoped some signal upstairs wasn't tipping off a guard that they were coming.

A *ping* sounded for Floor One, and the doors ground open to reveal another small parking garage. The black limousine sat directly in front of the elevator doors, ready to move out when needed.

Angrily, Joe punched Three. "It makes sense that Cutter would live on top."

But when the door opened on Floor Three, they saw immediately that this choice was wrong. Avocado green indoor-outdoor carpet led away from the elevator. Frank clearly remembered a plush, cream-colored pile—the luxurious surroundings that Daniel Cutter cultivated.

"I don't believe it." Joe pounded on the elevator wall as the doors slid closed, and Frank pushed the button labeled Two.

It was evidence of Cutter's faith in his ingenious hideaway that there was no guard in the hall on Floor Two. Frank, Joe, and Selden Brookshier moved silently into the hall, looked both ways, and headed down the hall to the right. A murmur of voices floated out the second door they came to. Frank motioned to Joe, who slid in front of the doorway. The threesome poised to listen.

"I knew you'd come to your senses, Annie." It was Cutter's voice, cold, sinister, mocking. "Too bad you held out for so long. Wouldn't it have been easier on you to have just led us to the diamonds without all this fuss?"

"You slime." Annie's voice was shaky, but angry still.

"Greedy people never win, Annie. Your share of the three million would have been generous, and with Phil out of the way, you could have had a percentage of his cut. You took care of him for us, so you earned it. He was scum. I usually don't hire such lowlifes, but I was careless this time.

"You're a strong and beautiful woman, Annie Shea. Not only could you have parlayed your cut into a bigger bankroll, but you could have kept working for us. The pay goes up with every successful job. Who knows, with your looks and polish, I might have taken a special interest in you."

"Over my dead body," Annie said with steel in her voice.

Cutter laughed. "Yes, you make it easy for me to believe that."

Frank kept one eye on Joe. He had been known to make some impulsive moves in the past, and Frank knew his emotions were involved here.

Anger at Cutter and his men wouldn't help Joe think rationally.

Annie spoke again. "Phil Sidler reminded me of one thing, Cutter. No one in this world can be trusted. I'll take *you* to the diamonds. By now, I'd think you might have some qualms about trusting any of your hoodlums with three million dollars."

There was a moment of silence. "You may have a point there, young lady, but you realize I've created this sanctuary for one reason. The world was never that kind to me. Here I am surrounded by everything I desire. Comfortable settings, excellent food—I have a chef I brought from Belgium, remarkable man. Some of the works of art—you no doubt haven't had time to enjoy them—would cause heart palpitations to any museum curator. I have a theater, a pool, a gym. Anything I desire is brought to me. Why should I go out into polluted air, traffic—the real world?"

"Because you want those diamonds. And those are my conditions," Annie answered.

"I hardly think you are in any position to dictate the conditions, Annie. But I admire your guts. As I said, it's a shame—"

"I'm willing to die before I tell you," Annie said, her voice getting stronger.

Joe crossed back to Frank. "She's on our side, Frank, I know she is. No matter what you've

heard. She's getting Cutter out of here for us."
Joe's voice was the slightest whisper, but Frank
signaled for absolute silence.

"Novel idea." Cutter paused, no doubt to think
about Annie's ultimatum. "I haven't been outside
for years. Perhaps I should see if it's still as bad
as I remember."

There was a long pause before Cutter added,
"Oh, and, Annie, if you don't deliver this time,
only one of us will come back alive."

Chapter

16

BROOKSHIER SQUEEZED FRANK'S arm and tapped Joe on the shoulder. He motioned in the direction of the elevator. Joe shook his head. Brookshier insisted. Frank caught on. They had to get off this floor before Cutter made his move. They had no hope of capturing the gang on their own turf. They were outmanned and unarmed except for Brookshier's Beretta.

In addition, if Annie did have the diamonds and could persuade Cutter to go with her to where she'd hidden them, they could catch him with the evidence they needed to put him away for years. Put him in an equally isolated environment, but one where he might miss his little luxuries.

In the elevator Frank punched Ground Floor and willed the huge cage to move so they could escape ahead of Cutter's gang. Cutter would certainly bring along adequate protection for his venture into the real world.

"She's getting him out. Good for her." Brookshier slammed his fist on the palm of his left hand. "She's going to lead him to the diamonds, and we'll be right there with them."

Joe, Frank, and Brookshier dashed from the elevator the minute it opened. They crowded into Callie's car.

"What happened?" Callie asked. She had the engine running the minute she saw the trio head for her.

"Shut off the car," ordered Joe, "and get down. But be ready to move out when we tell you."

"Annie's inside," Frank explained, hunched in the front seat beside Callie. "She told them she has the diamonds, but she's talked Cutter into going with her to get them."

"They should be right behind us." Joe and Brookshier were tucked into the backseat.

In no time the elevator door rumbled open and the sleek, black limo purred, its engine barely humming. As it sped up the ramp into the New York City street, Callie flicked on the ignition. Her car sprang to life and she pulled out, pursuing them.

"Maybe you'd better keep low," she said to her passengers. "If anyone is watching out the back, they'll never suspect that I'm following them.''

"Good thinking, Callie.'' Frank smiled at her from his slumped-down position. "You do come in handy sometimes.''

"When this is over, Frank Hardy, you're treating me to the best dinner in Bayport. It's not every day I risk my life for you.''

Her smile was warm, and Frank knew she liked being in on the action. "It's a deal, Callie.''

The limo drove the speed limit, smoothly and skillfully negotiating the city streets and pulling onto the expressway.

"Hey, we're heading for Bayport,'' Joe said, peeking out the back window.

"I knew it,'' said Brookshier. "I knew Annie had the diamonds or knew where they were hidden, and I had a feeling they were in Bayport.''

"What would Annie Shea do with three million dollars' worth of diamonds?'' asked Callie. "I sure wouldn't know what to do with them. You can't spend diamonds.''

"She may not have planned beyond taking them.'' Brookshier wiggled, trying to get comfortable in the small, narrow backseat. His tall frame didn't fold up easily. "You have to have the kind of connections Cutter obviously has to convert them to cash.''

"I wouldn't trust anyone if I had them,'' Callie said. "If you don't know where to sell them, you might as well not steal them. Annie is pretty naïve."

Joe said nothing. Everyone in the car—except for him—seemed to have accepted the fact that Annie was a thief.

Callie had no trouble following the limo all the way to the airport, and apparently no one in the dark car suspected that she was tailing them. "Look, guys. We're headed for the Bayport mall."

Frank sat up cautiously. "They're pulling up to the delivery door of Mr. Pizza. I wish there were some way to warn Tony to clear out his kitchen and the restaurant. We don't want anyone hurt."

"I'll go in the front door," offered Callie.

"Call the police while you're there, Callie," Frank instructed. "Ask for Officer O'Hara or Con Riley. Tell them to get over here on the double. We don't want to give Cutter a chance to escape now that we have him with evidence. Better tell them to find our dad, too."

"I don't want Annie hurt," Joe said in a low voice. "Whatever she's done, there must be an explanation."

Frank hated to say that if Annie had stolen the diamonds there couldn't be any way to justify it— and there was still the unsolved mystery of Phil Sidler's death. Cutter's words came to Frank:

"Thanks for getting rid of Phil Sidler for us, Annie." What did that mean?

Callie parked as close as she dared to the limo. Quickly her passengers slid out. Then she drove around to the front of the mall before the others got inside.

Frank, Joe, and Brookshier watched as Cutter, dressed as he'd been when they'd seen him, including his diamond ring, stepped from the black car, flanked by two of his bodyguards. He looked around cautiously, probably feeling very vulnerable away from his sanctuary. Another man gripped Annie's arm, as if they thought her plan might be to escape from them here instead of leading them to the diamonds.

Tony Prito had obviously locked the storeroom door that day. "But look, Annie has a key," said Joe.

Sure enough, Annie had searched through her purse, then lifted out a key and prepared to slip it into the lock. She dropped the key, and as she bent to retrieve it, she made her move. Chopping across her guard's neck with one hand, she grabbed his gun and leaped forward. She took Cutter by the arm and spun him around, shoving the gun in his back. No one had suspected she'd make such a move, and they were all caught off guard.

For a moment Joe and Frank, along with Brookshier, stood frozen, watching. But as Annie inched toward the storeroom door with Cutter as hostage, Joe leaped forward, running for the pair.

"Good work, Annie. I knew you had a plan."

Taking one of Cutter's bodyguards by surprise, Joe twisted him around and kicked the gun from his hand. Frank, never one to hang back when Joe made a move, disarmed the other man in a similar way.

Annie's face, bruised and swollen from the beating she'd taken, registered surprise, but not for long. "I should have trusted you more, Joe," she said, smiling gratefully at him. "I thought you'd stopped looking for me. Let's get these crooks packaged up nicely, and then call the authorities." Whipping out a scarf from her purse, Annie started to tie Cutter's hands behind his back.

"You're a fool, Annie," Cutter growled. "You think they'll let you go, even if you turn me in? Get the diamonds and we'll leave together. I'll show you a life you never even dreamed possible." Cutter's sunglasses had fallen to the ground during his scuffle with Annie. His eyes glared out evilly from the scars on his face.

Annie laughed. "What's that, Cutter? Locked up in your ivory tower? No thanks. I like beaches and sun and tropical waters too much to live like a recluse."

Joe and Frank slipped the belts off their pants to make sure Cutter's two bodyguards were bound and didn't go anyplace until the police arrived.

Brookshier checked out the man Annie had karate-chopped. He was still out cold. "The diamonds, Annie. Where are they?" That was his main concern. He'd let the police deal with the crooks. "We'll need them as evidence against Cutter. With them and your testimony, we'll put him away for a long time."

Annie smiled and backed closer to the storeroom door of Mr. Pizza, still holding the gun. "What are they worth to you? I kind of liked knowing I held a fortune in my hand." Slipping the key she had retrieved from the step into the lock, she swung open the door and paused in the doorway.

"We might be able to make a deal for you, Annie," said Brookshier. "Or maybe the reward for returning stolen goods will pay for a good lawyer. You were instrumental in capturing Cutter. That should count for something. We've been after him for some time."

"Don't listen to him, Annie," Cutter growled. "He won't get you any deal. There's still time for us to leave together."

Annie's eyes, sparkling with excitement, met Joe's disillusioned gaze. For a moment, as their eyes met, the girl's tough demeanor wavered, her triumphant smile faltered. She frowned at Joe and looked away.

"Give me the gun, Annie." Frank stepped closer to the red-haired girl. "Joe and I will help you all we can."

"I wish I could trust you, Frank. I know you mean well." For the first time Annie almost smiled at Frank. She held the gun comfortably, the cold steel no stranger to the palm of her hand.

"You have to trust someone, Annie." Joe inched closer.

"All right, Joe." She looked him full in the face now. She seemed to have made up her mind about something. "You. You reach into that barrel of flour." Annie motioned Joe past her and into the storeroom. She stayed in the doorway, her gun on Frank and Brookshier. "That's right, that one. The bag is buried near the bottom." She laughed. "I didn't want some pizza customer thinking they'd won the prize in a box of Cracker Jacks."

Joe leaned over and sifted his fingers deeper and deeper into the cardboard barrel of flour. Finally he stood up, having retrieved a small cloth sack with a drawstring at the top. He came back to Annie and, opening it, took out a handful of uncut diamonds, most of which were the size of a kid's marbles.

Frank whistled. One of the uncut gems was as large as the one in Cutter's ring. It was probably worth a million by itself. But Brookshier was right. Where would Annie have fenced a marble sack full of shiny rocks?

He looked at Brookshier, whose eyes were on the diamonds, the "sight" he was being paid to recover.

Joe, who stood closest to Annie, was too mesmerized by the gems to think for a moment. And before Frank could decide what to do, Annie called the next shot.

"Thanks, Joe." She snatched the bag as soon as Joe tumbled the rocks back into it and pulled the opening shut. At the same time the gun in her hand pushed into the small of Joe's back. "And if you don't mind, I'll need you for a little longer."

With those words she pulled Joe backward toward the door into the pizza restaurant. The problem of turning the stolen diamonds into cash didn't seem to matter to her.

She had the hostage she needed to escape.

Chapter

17

"ANNIE, DON'T DO this," Joe pleaded. "You trapped Cutter for us. That'll go a long way toward getting you a lighter sentence. You might even get probation."

"You really don't understand, do you, Joe?"

"I understand that I liked you, Annie. I can't believe you're doing this." Joe pulled away from Annie and leaned on a counter in the deserted pizza storeroom. He didn't think Annie would actually shoot him.

She kept her gun pointed at him, however. "I'm sorry it had to be you I'm taking hostage, Joe. But I certainly don't want to take Cutter with me to Rio. I lured him here because I wanted him and his men out of my way."

A sadness invaded Joe's whole being. Boy, he

thought bitterly, I really know how to choose 'em.

Maybe Annie sensed his feelings. "I'm sorry, Joe," she said again. "But you have to understand—this is my one chance to make it big. You don't know what it's like to grow up poor. I saw the home you were raised in. I know your type. You're the kind of guy who would never even look at me in high school because I was from the wrong side of town."

"This is not the way out, Annie. Even if you got to Rio and sold the diamonds, what would your life be like always running? Sooner or later you'd be caught."

Annie laughed a derisive laugh. The bright smile Joe liked so much had deserted her face now, leaving a bitter, hard expression he had never seen before. "Who cares? At least I'd have a good life until then."

"You could start over right here." Joe moved toward Annie.

"Stay away from me, Joe. I don't want to have to hurt you." Annie waved the gun. "But I will if you don't cooperate."

"Don't you care for me at all, Annie?" Joe asked. He needed to know that he hadn't been taken in totally by this beautiful girl. He needed to know that her optimism and courage, all the qualities he'd seen in her, were real, not lies she had fed him. And that her affection for him wasn't an act she'd put on to cover up what she was doing.

Annie stared at Joe for a minute. "Of course I do, Joe. I like you a lot. If—if things had been different . . ." Annie took a deep breath. "But they aren't." If Annie's toughness was an act, it was a good one. Her voice hardened, and she motioned for Joe to step in front of her. She was ready to make her move.

"Annie, when we got here, Callie went to call the police. They'll have the entire place surrounded by now. There's no possibility of your getting away." Joe made one more attempt at talking sense into Annie, into persuading her to give herself up.

"I'm sure the police, your father, Frank—all the people who are out there, Joe—value your life. They'll let me go since you'll be with me."

Joe shrugged and tried to harden his heart toward Annie. He needed to concentrate on getting away from her with neither of them getting hurt. In spite of everything, he couldn't stand to see Annie killed or injured. Silently he settled on a simple plan that he hoped would work.

The pizza restaurant was empty when they entered it. Callie and Tony had silently cleared everyone from the place. As they moved around tables and toward the front door, Annie clutched Joe's arm tighter and kept her gun jammed into his side. Slowly they inched their way toward the parking lot.

"How are you going to get to the airport, Annie?" Joe asked. If he could keep her talking, he might distract her easier.

"You're going to drive me, Joe. It'll be my last ride in your van."

"The van's out in the woods still. We'll have to borrow a car." Joe said whatever came into his head as he tensed himself for what was coming.

"Whatever you say, Joe. You know, you could go with me."

"No, Annie. I can't. It wouldn't work. I'll help you get away if I have to, but I won't go with you." Joe kept talking.

"Joe, are you all right?" Frank called as Joe and Annie stepped outside the mall into the parking lot.

The lot was full of police officers and spectators, although the police officers were trying to keep the onlookers pushed back. Fenton Hardy stood beside Frank, the two of them watching, wondering what to do.

"I'm fine, Frank," Joe called loudly, trying to act casual and put the police at ease. "I'm taking the Nova to help Annie get to the airport, but wait for me before you go to dinner, Frank. I'm practically *faint* with hunger."

Frank's eyes widened for a second as he realized that Joe was trying to send him a message. He shouted back, "That figures. Will do." And he smiled, a little nervously. Whatever Joe had planned, his smile said, Frank would try to play along.

"Shut up, Joe," Annie said, poking him with the barrel of her gun and glancing at the policemen. "You're making me nervous. I'm sure you don't want me nervous with this gun in your back and my finger on the trigger."

Joe stopped talking, but when they were as close to Frank as they were going to get, he made his move. Suddenly he melted into a dead faint at Annie's feet.

At the same time, he rolled into her, pushing her backward and off balance. Her finger squeezed the trigger of the gun she held, but since her gun was pointed into the air, the shot zipped off harmlessly.

Frank was ready. He sprinted toward the pair. But just as he reached for Annie's gun, she regained her balance and took a step back, giving herself a split second in which to shoot.

As Frank's momentum propelled him forward toward the weapon, he looked up at Annie. Tense and trembling, she had the gun aimed at Frank's chest and her finger on the trigger. Her eyes met Frank's. In that instant he knew that no matter how much Annie wanted the diamonds and her freedom, she couldn't shoot the gun.

"Annie," Joe said off to the side. When she turned to him, Frank quickly chopped at her arm and she dropped the weapon. Then it was only a matter of Joe and Frank holding on to her, not an easy task, since she fought like a wild woman.

Officer O'Hara closed in with handcuffs. With her arms pinned, Annie finally realized she had lost.

It was a quiet foursome who stood at the police station after all the formalities had been taken care of. Cutter and his men were behind bars. Annie had surrendered the diamonds, and they would be handed over to Selden Brookshier, who would return them to the manufacturer who had ordered them.

Brookshier thanked the Hardys for their help on the case and apologized for treating them so roughly.

"We must avoid publicity in these cases, you understand," he said again, trying to justify his methods. "That's why I had to hit and run from the start. It's vital that not too many people know that millions of dollars' worth of diamonds are delivered all over the country every day. As far as Annie goes—well, you see I had to scare her to get her to lead me to the jewels."

Officer O'Hara made her way to where Callie, Frank, Joe, and Fenton Hardy stood. "Joe," she said with some difficulty, "I guess I owe you an apology." She put out her hand. Joe took it with no hard feelings. "Before I met you and your brother, I had the idea that teenagers couldn't be trusted. I guess I'd better revise my thinking."

"What about the charges against Joe?" Fenton Hardy asked.

"They've all been dropped," Officer O'Hara said. "Annie finally told us the whole story, clearing Joe. Phil Sidler was already dead when Annie pushed him in front of the van Joe was driving."

"Annie killed him?" Frank said in an astonished voice. He had figured out that Annie pushed Phil, but not that she'd killed him first.

"She had a gun in her purse," O'Hara explained. "She hit him in the back of the head with it. Then she pushed him so it would look like Joe ran over him."

"Those staring eyes." Joe's face, already grim, showed even greater grief. Although he was glad to hear the charges against him were dropped, he didn't want to hear that Annie was a murderer.

"I think she may have even planned it, Joe," Officer O'Hara said. "She definitely meant from the beginning to set you up. She's a regular Black Widow. I'm arresting her for first-degree murder."

Joe shook his head in utter disbelief, but said nothing.

"Joe, she asked if she could see you again," Officer O'Hara said. "It's all right with me if you want to see her."

Joe hesitated. Then he shook his head slowly again. "No—I don't want to see her."

"I think this case is finished," said Frank, taking Joe's arm. "Let's get out of here, Joe."

Frank steered Joe toward the front door of the police station after taking the car keys that Callie slipped into his hand. He smiled at her gratefully, knowing she understood that he and Joe needed time alone.

In the lot they climbed into the car and sat quietly for a minute. Joe stared into space, utterly exhausted.

"Want something to eat, little brother?" Frank asked, starting the engine.

"It's funny," Joe said in a quiet voice. "I really am hungry. But I don't want pizza."

"Fine, pizza it's not. I'll surprise you."

"I may never eat pizza again. And remind me of one thing, Frank." Joe looked out the window at the growing darkness. "Not even to *look* at the waitress."

Joe spoke in a flippant manner, but Frank knew the remark covered a lot of pain. He also knew the pain would stay with Joe for a long time.

"Good idea, partner. We need to keep our minds on business anyway. And food. How does this sound: double cheeseburgers, fries, extra-creamy chocolate malts?"

"Mind-boggling." Joe smiled wearily.

Frank and Joe's next case:

Frank and Joe go undercover as big-city bicycle messengers to crack a gang of high-tech thieves. Millions of dollars in computer secrets have already been stolen, and the brother detectives are hot on the trail.

Zipping through New York traffic at top speeds is dangerous enough, but one of their fellow messengers is out for their blood. As suspects become victims and leads turn into red herrings, the Hardys roll into action in the fast lane . . . in *Street Spies,* Case #21 in The Hardy Boys Casefiles™.